BETWEEN FRIENDS

Ariella, unhappy in love, confides in the woman whose husband she stole; Nahum, a devoted father, can't find the words to challenge his daughter's promiscuous lover; the old idealists deplore the apathy of the young, while the young are so used to kibbutz life that they can't work out if they're impassioned or indifferent. And amid this, Martin attempts to teach Esperanto. At the heart of each drama is a desire to be better, more principled, and worthy of the community's respect. Amos Oz leaves us with the feeling that what matters the most between friends is the invisible tie of our shared humanity.

SPECIAL  DERS

THE ULVERSCROFT FOUNDATION
(registered UK charity number 264873)
was established in 1972 to provide funds for
research, diagnosis and treatment of eye diseases.
Examples of major projects funded by
the Ulverscroft Foundation are:-

- The Children's Eye Unit at Moorfields Eye Hospital, London
- The Ulverscroft Children's Eye Unit at Great Ormond Street Hospital for Sick Children
- Funding research into eye diseases and treatment at the Department of Ophthalmology, University of Leicester
- The Ulverscroft Vision Research Group, Institute of Child Health
- Twin operating theatres at the Western Ophthalmic Hospital, London
- The Chair of Ophthalmology at the Royal Australian College of Ophthalmologists

You can help further the work of the Foundation
by making a donation or leaving a legacy.
Every contribution is gratefully received. If you
would like to help support the Foundation or
require further information, please contact:

THE ULVERSCROFT FOUNDATION
The Green, Bradgate Road, Anstey
Leicester LE7 7FU, England
Tel: (0116) 236 4325

website: www.foundation.ulverscroft.com

AMOS OZ

BETWEEN FRIENDS

Complete and Unabridged

ULVERSCROFT
Leicester

First published in Great Britain in 2013 by
Chatto & Windus
London

First Large Print Edition
published 2014
by arrangement with
Chatto & Windus
The Random House Group Limited
London

A catalogue record for this book is available
from the British Library.

ISBN 978–1–4448–1969–4

Published by
F. A. Thorpe (Publishing)
Anstey, Leicestershire

Set by Words & Graphics Ltd.
Anstey, Leicestershire
Printed and bound in Great Britain by
T. J. International Ltd., Padstow, Cornwall

This book is printed on acid-free paper

Contents

The King of Norway

On our kibbutz, Kibbutz Yekhat, there lived a man, Zvi Provizor, a short fifty-five-year-old bachelor who had a habit of blinking. He loved to transmit bad news: earthquakes, plane crashes, buildings collapsing on their occupants, fires and floods. He read the papers and listened to all the news broadcasts very early in the morning, so that he could catch us at the entrance to the dining hall and astound us with the story of two hundred and fifty coal miners hopelessly trapped somewhere in China, or six hundred passengers drowned when a ferry capsized in a storm in the Caribbean. He also used to memorise obituaries. Always first to know which famous people had died, he would inform the entire kibbutz. One morning he stopped me on the path in front of the clinic.

'Ever hear of a writer named Wislavsky?'

'Yes. Why?'

'He died.'

'Sorry to hear it.'

'Writers die too.'

And another time he caught me when I was working the dining-hall shift: 'I saw in the

3

obituaries that your grandfather died.'

'Yes.'

'And three years ago, your other grand-father died.'

'Yes.

'So this one was the last.'

Zvi Provizor was the kibbutz gardener. He would go out at five every morning, reposition the sprinklers, till the soil in the flower beds, plant and prune and water, mow lawns with the noisy mower, spray against aphids, and spread organic and chemical fertiliser. Attached to his belt was a small transistor radio that provided him with a constant infusion of disastrous news: 'Did you hear? A huge massacre in Angola.'

Or: 'The Minister of Religious Affairs died. They just announced it ten minutes ago.'

The other kibbutz members avoided him. In the dining hall, they rarely joined him at his table. On summer evenings he would sit alone on the green bench at the foot of the large lawn in front of the dining hall and watch the children playing on the grass. The breeze billowed out his shirt, drying his sweat. A hot summer moon shone red as it rose above the tall cypress trees. One evening Zvi Provizor greeted a woman named Luna Blank who was sitting alone on an adjacent bench.

'Did you hear?' he said to her sadly, 'In Spain an orphanage burned down and eighty orphans died of smoke inhalation.'

Luna, a forty-five-year-old widowed teacher, wiped the perspiration from her brow with a handkerchief and said, 'That's horrible.'

'Only three survivors were rescued,' Zvi said, 'and they're in a critical condition.'

We all respected his dedication to his work: never, in the twenty-two years that he'd lived on the kibbutz, had a single sick day been noted on his time sheet. Thanks to him, the kibbutz bloomed. Every unused strip of land was planted with seasonal flowers. Here and there he had put in rock gardens where he planted varieties of cactus. He had erected wooden trellises for grapevines. In front of the dining hall he installed a burbling fountain filled with goldfish and aquatic plants. He had a good aesthetic sense and everyone appreciated it.

But behind his back we called him the Angel of Death and gossiped about him: he didn't have and had never had an interest in women, we would say. Or in men, for that matter. One young fellow, Roni Shindlin, did a marvellous imitation of Zvi that made us roar with laughter. In the afternoon, when the kibbutz members sat on their porches and drank coffee or played with their children on the small lawns in front of their houses, Zvi Provizor would go to the clubhouse to read the newspapers in the company of five or six solitary men like him, avid readers and debaters, aging bachelors, widowers or divorceés.

From his corner, Reuvkeh Roth, a small bald man with large batlike ears, would mumble that retaliatory raids only escalated the violence because revenge begets revenge and retaliation begets retaliation.

The others would immediately attack him: 'What are you talking about? We can't let them get away with it!' 'Restraint and appeasement only make the Arabs more brazen.'

Zvi Provizor would blink and say, 'In the end, it'll turn into a war. It can only cause a terrible war.'

And Emanuel Glozman, the stutterer, would say excitedly, 'W-w-war. Very g-g-good. We'll w-w-win and t-t-take their l-l-land all the w-w-way to the J-J-Jordan.'

Reuvkeh Roth would think out loud, 'Ben Gurion is a great chess player. He always sees five moves ahead. Except that everything with him is always by force.'

On that subject, Zvi Provizor would prophesy gloomily, 'If we lose, the Arabs will come and wipe us out. If we win, the Russians will come and blow us up.'

Emanuel Glozman would plead, 'E-e-enough,

friends, qu-qu-quiet. Let m-m-me read the p-p-papers in p-p-peace.'

And Zvi, after a few moments' silence, would say, 'Did you hear? It says here that the King of Norway has liver cancer. And the head of our regional council has cancer, too.'

Whenever Roni Shindlin, the comedian, saw Zvi at the shoemaker's or by the clothing storeroom, he would ask him mockingly, 'So, Angel of Death, what plane crashed today?'

★ ★ ★

Zvi Provizor and Luna Blank fell into a routine: they talked every evening. He would sit on the right-hand edge of the left bench at the foot of the lawn and she would sit near him, on the left-hand edge of the right bench. He would blink as he spoke to her and she, wearing a pretty, sleeveless sundress, would crumple her handkerchief between her fingers. Praising the kibbutz gardens, the fruit of his labour, she said that thanks to him they lived on a green meadow, in the shade of blossoming orchards, among blooming flower beds. She had a weakness for fancy words. A third-grade teacher, she made excellent, delicate pencil drawings that hung on the walls of our small apartments. Her face was round and smiling and her eyelashes long, though her neck was slightly wrinkled and she had thin legs and almost no breasts. Her husband had been killed several years earlier while doing reserve duty on the Gaza border and they'd had no children. The kibbutz members considered her an admirable figure, a woman who had overcome tragedy and poured her entire soul into teaching. Zvi talked to her about the different species of roses and she nodded eagerly, as if agreeing with every word. Then he gave her a detailed description of the horrors of the locust plague that was devastating Sudan.

Luna said, 'You're a very sensitive person.'

Zvi blinked rapidly and said, 'Sudan doesn't have much greenery as it is.'

Luna said, 'Why do you take all the sorrows of the world on your shoulders?'

And Zvi replied, 'Closing your eyes to the cruelty of life is, in my opinion, both stupid and sinful. There's very little we can do about it. So we have to at least acknowledge it.'

★ ★ ★

One summer evening she invited Zvi to her place for coffee. He came in his after-work clothes, long khaki trousers and a short-sleeved light-blue shirt. His radio was still attached to his belt, and at eight o'clock he excused himself and listened to the news headlines. Hanging on the walls of Luna Blank's room were several of her pencil drawings in simple frames, sketches of dreamy young girls and landscapes, rocky hills and olive trees. Beneath the window was a double bed with embroidered oriental pillows. The row of books on the white bookshelf was arranged by height, from tall art books of paintings by Van Gogh, Cézanne and Gauguin, to shorter volumes of the Cassuto Bible and, finally, a series of squat little novels published by Hasifria Le'Am. In the middle of the room was a round coffee table with two plain armchairs on either side. The table was covered with an embroidered tablecloth and set for two with coffee cups and plates for biscuits.

Zvi Provizor said, 'Your room is very nice,' and added, 'Clean. Neat.'

Embarrassed, Luna Blank said, 'Thank you. I'm glad.'

But there was no gladness in her voice, only an awkward tension.

Then they drank coffee and ate biscuits and spoke of ornamental trees and fruit trees, of the discipline problems at school now that everything is permitted, of bird migration.

Zvi said, 'I read in the newspaper that in Hiroshima, ten years after the bomb, there were still no birds.'

Luna told him again, 'You take all the sorrows of the world on your shoulders.'

She also said, 'The day before yesterday I saw a hoopoe on a low branch outside my window.'

★　★　★

And so they began to meet regularly in the early evening hours, on a bench in the garden, in the shade of a dense bougainvillea, or over coffee in Luna's room. Zvi would come home from work at four, shower, comb his hair in front of the mirror, change into his ironed khaki trousers and light-blue shirt and go to join her. Sometimes he would bring seedlings of annuals for her to plant in her small garden. Once he brought her a volume of Yaakov Fichman's poems. She gave him poppy-seed biscuits in a bag, and a pencil drawing of two cypress trees and a bench. But at eight or eight-thirty they would say good-night and Zvi would return to his monastic room where the smell of bachelordom hung heavily in the air.

In the dining hall Roni Shindlin said that the Angel of Death had spread its wings over the Black Widow. In the clubhouse, later, Reuvkeh Roth teased Zvi affectionately, 'So the hand has found a glove, eh?'

But Zvi and Luna were not upset by the gossip and the sarcasm. The connection between them seemed to grow stronger every day. He told her that in his free time he was translating a novel by the Polish writer Iwaszkiewicz into Hebrew. The book was full of gentleness and suffering. Iwaszkiewicz believed that the human condition was absurd but touching. Luna listened, her head slightly tilted, lips parted, pouring hot coffee into his cup, as if the coffee were a kind of compensation for Iwaszkiewicz's sorrow as well as a consolation for his own. She felt that their relationship was precious and she appreciated the way it filled her days, which until then had been so flat and monotonous. One night, she dreamed that they were on a horse together, her breasts pressed against his back and her arms around his waist, riding along a valley between high hills where a frothing river twisted and turned. She decided not to tell Zvi about this dream, even though she had described other dreams to him in detail. Zvi, for his part, blinked and told her that as a child in the Polish town of Yanov, he had dreamed of being a student. Instead, he had been drawn into the newly formed *chalutz* youth movement and had given up his plans to study. Even so, he had never stopped learning. Carefully gathering

11

the crumbs from the tablecloth, Luna said, 'You must have been a very shy young man. You're still a bit shy now.'

Zvi said, 'You don't really know me.'

Luna said, 'Tell me. I'm listening.'

And Zvi said, 'Tonight I heard on the radio that a volcano erupted in Chile. Four villages were totally destroyed by the lava flow. Most of the people didn't stand a chance.'

One evening, as he regaled her with an affecting description of the famine in Somalia, compassion for him so overwhelmed her that she suddenly took his hand and held it to her breast. Zvi trembled and pulled his hand back quickly, with a gesture that was almost violent. His eyes blinked frantically. Never in his adult life had he touched another person intentionally, and he went rigid whenever he was touched. He loved the feel of loose earth and the softness of young stems, but the touch of others, men or women, caused his entire body to stiffen and contract as if he'd been burned. He always tried to avoid handshakes, pats on the back or the accidental rubbing of elbows at the table in the dining hall. A short time later, he stood up and left.

He didn't go to see Luna the next day. He had begun to feel that their relationship was heading towards a disastrous place where he did not want to go, a place that repulsed him.

Luna, with her usual sensitivity, guessed that she had somehow offended him. She decided to apologise, though she didn't know what for. Had she asked a question she shouldn't have asked? Or had she perhaps failed to grasp some important meaning concealed in his words?

Two days later, when he wasn't in his room, she slipped a note under his door: *I'm sorry if I upset you. Can we talk?*

Zvi responded with a note of his own: *It would be better if we didn't. It would only end badly.*

Still, she waited for him after supper at the foot of the margosa tree near the dining-hall door and said shyly, 'Tell me what I did.'

'Nothing.'

'So why are you avoiding me?'

'Try to understand. It's . . . pointless.'

They never met on purpose again, and if they happened to pass each other on a path or in the small storeroom, they would exchange nods, hesitate for a moment, then go on their way.

At lunch, Roni Shindlin told his table-mates that the Angel of Death had cut his honeymoon short and, from now on, they were all in danger again. In fact, that very afternoon Zvi informed the bachelors in the clubhouse that a large bridge in Turkey had collapsed, and at the height of rush hour to boot.

Two or three months later we noticed that Luna Blank had stopped coming to the classical-music group and had even been absent from several teachers' meetings. She dyed her hair a coppery red and began to wear bright lipstick. Occasionally she skipped supper. On the Sukkoth holiday she stayed in the city for a few days and came back wearing a dress we thought was a bit daring, with a long slit up the side. In early autumn we saw her a few times, sitting on the bench by the large lawn with the basketball coach, a man ten years younger than she was, who came to the kibbutz twice a week. Roni Shindlin said that she was probably learning to dribble at night. Two or three weeks later, she dropped the basketball coach and was seen in the company of the commander of the kibbutz unit of the Fighting Pioneer Youth, a man of twenty-two. There was no way that this could be ignored, and the Education Committee met discreetly to discuss the professional implications.

Every evening, Zvi Provizor would sit alone, utterly still, on the bench next to the fountain he had installed with his own hands and watch the children playing on the lawn. If you passed by and said good evening, he would return the greeting and tell you about the floods in south-eastern China.

Late that autumn, without warning and

14

without permission from the kibbutz secretariat, Luna Blank left for America to visit her sister, who had sent her a plane ticket. She was seen one morning at the bus stop wearing the daring dress and a bright-coloured scarf, teetering in high heels and lugging a large suitcase. 'Already dressed for Hollywood,' Roni Shindlin said. 'The Black Widow is fleeing the Angel of Death.' The secretariat decided to suspend her membership in the kibbutz, pending further investigation.

Meanwhile, Luna Blank's room remained locked and dark, even though there was a housing shortage and some members of the Housing Committee had their eye on it. Five or six ordinary houseplants — philodendrons, geraniums, cacti — had been left on the small porch and Zvi Provizor would occasionally go by to water and tend to them.

Then came winter. Low clouds lay above the ornamental trees. Thick mud lined the fields and orchards, and the fruit-pickers and field-hands went to work in the factory. Grey rain fell endlessly. At night the gutters rattled noisily and a cold wind seeped through cracks in the shutters. Zvi Provizor sat up every night listening to all the news broadcasts, and in the breaks between them he'd bend over his table and by the light of his gooseneck lamp translate into Hebrew a few lines of

Iwaszkiewicz's anguish-filled novel. The pencil drawing that Luna had given him — two cypress trees and a bench — hung above his bed. The trees looked melancholy, the bench was empty. At ten-thirty he'd wrap something round himself and go out onto the porch to look at the low-lying clouds and the deserted concrete paths, their wet surfaces gleaming in the yellow glow of the streetlight. If there was a pause between downpours, he would take a brief nocturnal stroll to see how the plants on Luna's porch were doing. Fallen leaves had already covered the step, and Zvi thought that he could detect the light scent of soap or shampoo drifting from inside the locked room. He would wander along the empty paths for a while, rain dripping from the tree branches onto his uncovered head, then go back to his room and listen in darkness, his open eyes blinking, to the final news reports of the day. Early one morning, when everything was still blanketed in wet, frozen darkness, he stopped a dairy-worker on his way to milk the cows and informed him sadly:

'Did you hear? The King of Norway died last night. Cancer. Of the liver.'

Two Women

Early in the morning, before sunrise, the cooing of pigeons in the bushes begins to drift through her open window. The throaty sound, steady and unbroken, soothes her. A light breeze blows across the tops of the pine trees and a cock crows on the slope of the hill. A dog barks in the distance and another one answers it. Those sounds wake Osnat before the alarm clock rings, and she gets out of bed, turns off the alarm, showers and puts on her work clothes. At five-thirty she leaves for her job in the kibbutz laundry. On the way she passes Boaz and Ariella's apartment, which looks locked and dark. They must still be sleeping, she thinks, and that thought stirs neither jealousy nor pain in her, only a vague disbelief: as if everything that happened had not happened to her but to strangers, and not two months ago, but many years before. In the laundry she switches on the electric light because the daylight is still too faint. Then she bends over the waiting piles of laundry and begins to separate white from coloured and cotton from synthetic. Sour body odours rise from the dirty clothes, mingling with the smell of soap powder. Osnat works here alone, but she keeps her radio on all day to ease the solitude, though the humming of the washing machines muffles both the words and the music. At seven-thirty she completes the first round, empties the machines and reloads them, then goes to the dining hall for breakfast. She always walks slowly, as if she's not sure where she wants to go or doesn't care. Here, on our kibbutz, Osnat is considered a very quiet girl.

At the beginning of the summer, Boaz told Osnat he's been in a relationship with Ariella Barash for eight months and has decided that the three of them cannot go on living a lie. So he's made up his mind to leave Osnat and move his things to Ariella's apartment. 'You're not a little girl anymore,' he says. 'You know, Osnat, that things like this happen every day now all over the world, and on our kibbutz too. Luckily, we don't have children. It could have been a lot harder for us.' He'll take his bicycle with him but leave the radio for her. He wants the separation to be as amicable as their life together has been for all these years. He completely understands if she's angry with him. Even though she doesn't really have anything to be angry about: 'The relationship with Ariella wasn't meant to hurt you. Things like this just happen, that's all.' In any case, he's sorry. He'll move his things out right away and leave her not only the radio but everything else, including the albums, the embroidered pillows and the coffee set they received as a wedding gift.

Osnat says, 'Yes.'

'What do you mean, 'Yes'?'

'Go,' she says. 'Just go.'

★   ★   ★

Ariella Barash was a tall, slim divorcée with a slender neck, cascading hair and laughing eyes, one of which had a slight squint. She worked in the chicken coop and was also head of the kibbutz Culture Committee, responsible for organising holidays, ceremonies and weddings. In addition, she was in charge of inviting lecturers for Friday nights and ordering movies for Wednesday-night showings in the dining hall. She had an old cat and a young dog, almost a puppy, which lived together peaceably in her apartment. The dog was frightened of the cat, and would politely give it a wide berth. The old cat would ignore the dog and walk past as if it were invisible. The two of them spent most of the day dozing in Ariella's apartment, the cat on the sofa and the dog on the rug,

21

indifferent to one another.

Ariella had been married for a year to a career army officer, Ephraim, who left her for a young woman soldier. Her relationship with Boaz began when he came to her apartment one day wearing a sweaty work singlet stained with machine oil. She'd asked him to drop by to fix a dripping tap. He had on a wide leather belt with a large metal buckle. As he bent over the tap, she stroked his sunburned back gently several times until he turned round without putting down his screwdriver and wrench. Since then he'd been sneaking into her apartment for half an hour here or an hour there, but there were those on Kibbutz Yekhat who noticed the sneaking around and did not keep that discovery to themselves. People on our kibbutz said, 'What a strange pair; he hardly says a word and she never shuts up.' Roni Shindlin, the comedian, said, 'The honey is eating the bear.' No one told Osnat about it, but her friends showered her with affection and found ways to remind her that she wasn't alone, if she needed anything, the slightest thing, and so on and so forth.

Then Boaz loaded his clothes into his bicycle basket and moved to Ariella's apartment. He'd come back in the afternoon from his job in the garage, take off his work clothes and go into the bathroom for his shower. From the doorway he'd always say to her, 'So, anything happen today?' And Ariella would reply in surprise: 'What should've happened? Nothing happened. Take your shower and we'll have coffee.'

★   ★   ★

In her mailbox, which was on the far-left side of the mailbox cabinet near the entrance to the dining hall, Ariella found a folded note in Osnat's round, unhurried handwriting:

'Boaz always forgets to take his blood pressure pills. He needs to take them in the morning and at night before bed, and in the morning he has to take half a cholesterol pill. He shouldn't put black pepper or a lot of salt on his salads, and he should eat low-fat cheese and no steak. He's allowed fish and chicken, but not strongly spiced. And he shouldn't gorge himself on sweets. Osnat.

'P.S. He should drink less black coffee.'

Ariella Barash wrote a reply to Osnat in her sharply angled, nervous handwriting, and put it in her mailbox:

'Thank you. It was very decent of you to write to me. Boaz also has heartburn, but he says it's nothing. I'll try to do everything you ask, but he's not easy and he couldn't care less about his health. He couldn't care less about lots of things. You know. Ariella B.'

Osnat wrote:

'If you don't let him eat fried, sour or spicy foods, he won't have heartburn. Osnat.'

Ariella Barash replied several days later:

'I often ask myself, what did we do? He suppresses his feelings and mine keep changing. He tolerates my dog but can't stand the cat. When he comes home from the garage in the afternoon, he asks me, 'So what happened today?' Then he takes a shower, drinks some black coffee and sits down in my armchair to read the papers. When I tried giving him tea instead of coffee, he got angry and grumbled that I should stop trying to be his mother. Then he dozes in the chair, the papers fall on the floor, and he wakes up at seven to listen to the news on the radio. He pets the dog while he listens, mumbling some indistinct words of endearment. But if the cat should jump onto his lap asking for affection, he heaves him off with such disgust that I cringe. When I asked him to fix a stuck drawer, he not only fixed the drawer but also took apart and reassembled two wardrobe doors that squeaked, and asked with a laugh if he should fix the floor or the roof too. I ask myself what it was about him that attracted me and sometimes still does, but I have no clear answer. Even after his shower, his nails are black with machine oil and his hands are rough and scratched. And after he shaves there's still stubble on his chin. Maybe it's that constant dozing of his — even when he's awake he seems to be dozing — that tempts me to try and wake him. But I manage to wake him up for only a short while, you know how, and that doesn't always happen either. Not a day goes by when I don't think about you, Osnat, and despise myself and wonder if there can be any forgiveness for what I did to you. Sometimes I tell myself that maybe Osnat didn't really care so much, maybe she didn't love him? It's hard to know. You might think that I actually chose to do that to you. But we don't really have a choice. This whole business of attraction between a man and a woman seems suddenly strange and even a bit ridiculous. Do you think so too? If you had children, you and I would have suffered a lot more. And what about him? What does he actually feel? How can anybody tell? You know so well what he should and shouldn't eat. But do you know what he feels? Or whether he feels at all? I once asked him if he has any regrets and he said, 'Look, you can see for yourself that I'm here with you and not with her.' I want you to know, Osnat, that almost every night after he falls asleep, I lie awake in bed and look at the moonlight coming into our dark bedroom through the crack in the curtains and ask myself what would've happened if I'd been you. I'm drawn to your stillness. If only I could absorb some of that stillness. Sometimes I get up and dress and walk to the door, thinking that I'll go to you in the middle of the night and explain it all, but what can I explain? I stand on the porch for ten minutes, look up at the clear night sky, locate the Plough, then get undressed again and go back to lying awake in bed. He's snoring peacefully and I feel a sudden longing to be somewhere else entirely. Maybe even in your room with you. But please understand, this only happens to me at night when I'm lying awake and can't fall asleep and don't understand what happened or why, and I just feel such an intense closeness to you. I'd like to work in the laundry with you, for example. Just the two of us. I always carry both your short notes in my pocket and take them out to read over and over again. I want you to know how much I value every word you wrote and also, even more, how impressed I am by what you didn't write. People on the kibbutz talk about us. They're surprised at Boaz; they say that I just walked past, leaned down and plucked him away from you and that he, Boaz, couldn't care less about which apartment he goes to after work or which bed he sleeps in. Roni Shindlin winked at me near the office one day, grinned and said, 'So, Mona Lisa, still waters run deep, eh?' I didn't answer him and walked away in shame. Later, at home, I cried. Sometimes at night I cry, after he falls asleep, not because of him or not only because of him, but because of me and because of you. As if something bad and ugly happened to both of us that can't be fixed. Sometimes I ask him: 'What, Boaz?' And he says: 'Nothing.' I'm attracted to that blankness — as if he has nothing, as if he came straight from a desert of solitude. And then — but why am I telling you this? After all, it hurts you to hear it and I don't want to add to your pain. Just the opposite: I want to share your loneliness the way I wanted to touch his for a moment. It's almost one in the morning now, he's asleep, curled up in foetal position, the dog at his feet, and the cat is lying here on the table, his yellow eyes following the movement of my hand as I keep writing and writing by the light of a goose-necked lamp. I know it's pointless, that I have to stop writing, that you won't even read this note, which has stretched to four pages. You'll probably tear it up and throw it away. Maybe you'll think I've lost my mind, and I really have. Let's meet and talk? Not about Boaz's diet or the medicine he needs to take. (I really do try not to let him forget. I try, but don't always succeed. You know that stubbornness of his, which seems like disdain but is more like indifference.) We could talk about totally different things. Like the seasons of the year, for example, or even the star-filled sky of these summer nights: I'm interested in stars and nebulae. Maybe you are too? I'm waiting for you to write a note telling me what you think, Osnat. Two words will do. I'm waiting. Ariella B.'

★　★　★

To this letter, which was waiting in her mailbox, Osnat chose not to reply. She read it twice, folded it up and put it in a drawer. Now she's standing utterly still, looking out of her window. Three kittens are by the fence: one is busy biting its paw; another is crouching or maybe dozing, but with ears pricked suspiciously, as if catching a thin sound; and the third is chasing its tail, constantly falling over and rolling softly onto its back because it's so young. A gentle breeze is blowing, just enough to cool a cup of tea. Osnat moves away from the window and sits down on the sofa, back straight, hands on her knees, eyes closed. It'll be evening soon and she'll listen

28

to light music on the radio and read a book. Then she'll undress, fold her after-work clothes neatly, lay out tomorrow's work clothes, shower, get into bed and go to sleep. Her nights are dreamless now, and she wakes even before the alarm clock rings. The pigeons wake her.

Between Friends

In the early hours, the first rain of the season began to fall on the kibbutz houses, its fields and orchards. The fresh smell of damp earth and clean leaves filled the air. The rain rattled along the gutters and washed the dust off the red roofs and tin sheds. At dawn, a gentle mist enveloped the buildings, and the flowers in the gardens sparkled with beads of water. A redundant lawn sprinkler continued its sputtering. A child's wet red tricycle stood diagonally across a path. From the treetops came the sharp, astonished cries of birds.

The rain woke Nahum Asherov from a fitful sleep. For several moments after waking, he thought he heard tapping on the shutters as if someone had come to tell him something. He sat up in his bed and listened intently until he realised that the first rain had come. Today, he'd go there, sit Edna down, look her directly in the eyes and speak to her. About everything. And to David Dagan, too. He couldn't just let it pass.

But what could he actually say to him? Or to her?

Nahum Asherov, a widower of about fifty,

was Kibbutz Yekhat's electrician. Edna was his only remaining child after his older son Yishai had been killed a few years ago in a retaliatory raid. A strong-minded young woman, black-eyed and olive-skinned, she had turned seventeen in the spring and was a senior at the kibbutz school. Every afternoon she would come from the dorm room she shared with three other girls to visit her father. She would sit across from him in an armchair, hugging her shoulders as if she were always cold. Even in summer she would hug herself that way. She would stay with him for about an hour until dusk fell, would make coffee, prepare them a plate of peeled, sliced fruit, and they would chat quietly about the news on the radio or her studies, before she left to spend the rest of the evening with her friends, or perhaps without them. Nahum didn't know and didn't ask about her social life, and she didn't volunteer anything. He once heard something about a fleeting relationship with Dubi the lifeguard, but the rumour died down. He and his daughter never talked about themselves, except for superficial things. Edna would say, for example, 'You have to go to the clinic. I don't like that cough of yours.'

Nahum would say, 'We'll see. Maybe next week. This week we're installing a new generator in the brooder house at the chicken coop.'

Sometimes they would talk about music, which they both loved. Sometimes they didn't talk at all, but played Schubert on the old gramophone. They never spoke about the deaths of Edna's mother or brother. Nor did they bring up childhood memories, or future plans. They had an unspoken agreement not to touch on feelings, nor to touch each other. Not even lightly: not a hand on a shoulder, not the brush of fingers on an arm. Standing at the door, about to leave, Edna would say, 'Bye, Dad. Don't forget to go to the clinic. I'll come again tomorrow or the day after.' And Nahum would say, 'Yes. Stop by. And take care of yourself. See you later.'

In a few months, Edna, along with all her classmates, would be going into the army. Since she had taught herself Arabic, she would be serving in the Intelligence Corps.

Just a few days before the first rain, Kibbutz Yekhat had been shocked when Edna Asherov packed up her clothes and belongings, left the dorm and moved in with David Dagan, a teacher her father's age. David Dagan was one of the kibbutz founders and leaders, an articulate, solidly built man with powerful shoulders, a short, sinewy neck and a full, neatly trimmed moustache that was threaded with grey. He had a tendency to argue ironically and assertively in a deep voice. Almost everyone accepted his authority when it came to ideological issues, as well as to matters of daily life, mainly because he was endowed with razor-sharp logic and irresistible powers of persuasion. He would interrupt you in the middle of a sentence, put his hand warmly on your shoulder and say firmly: hang on, just give me a minute so we can set things straight. He was a devout Marxist, but he loved listening to cantorial music. For many years now, David Dagan had been the kibbutz history teacher. He changed lovers frequently and had six children with four different women from our kibbutz and others in the area.

David Dagan was about fifty and Edna, who had been his student the previous year, was only seventeen. No wonder the gossip swirled wildly around Roni Shindlin's regular table in the dining hall. Names like Abishag the Shunammite, Lolita and Bluebeard were tossed about. Yoskeh M. said that such a disgrace shook the very foundations of the school. How could it be — a teacher and his young student? They ought to convene an immediate meeting of the Education Committee. Yoskha disagreed: after all, you can't argue with love; anyway, we've always advocated free love here. And Rivka R. said:

36

how could she do something like this to her father, after all he's lost? Poor Nahum, he just won't be able to bear it.

'The entire young generation suddenly wants to go to college,' David Dagan said in his deep voice from his table in the dining hall. 'No one wants to work in the fields and orchards anymore.' Then he added harshly, 'We have to draw a line somewhere. Does anyone disagree?'

Although everyone in the kibbutz felt sorry for Nahum Asherov, no one spoke up. Behind Edna's and David Dagan's backs they said: it will end in tears. And they said: he is really, really out of line. He was always out of line when it came to women. And as for her, we're simply shocked.

Nahum said nothing. It seemed to him that everyone who passed him on the kibbutz paths wondered what he would do, or why he wasn't doing it: your daughter has been seduced; how can you keep silent? He tried in vain to find comfort in his progressive views of love and freedom. But sorrow, embarrassment and shame filled his heart. Every morning he would go to his workshop, fix electric lights and cookers, replace old plugs with new ones, repair broken appliances. He would go out to the yard, a long ladder over his shoulder, toolbox in hand, to perform his

37

duties, such as running a new power line to the kindergarten. Morning, noon and night he would appear in the dining hall to stand mutely in the queue at the serving counter, load his meal onto a tray and then sit down in a corner to eat, preferably in silence. He always sat in the same corner. People spoke to him gently, as if they were speaking to someone who was terminally ill, avoiding any mention or even hint of his problem, and he would answer briefly in his quiet, composed, slightly hoarse voice. To himself he said: one more day and I'll go and talk to her. And to him, too. After all, she's still just a child.

But time passed. Day after day, Nahum Asherov sat in the electrician's workshop, shoulders stooped, glasses sliding down his nose, working on the appliances in need of repair: electric kettles, radios, fans. He told himself: after work today, I will definitely go there. I'll talk to both of them. I'll say only one or two things, then I'll grab Edna's arm and drag her home. Not to her room in the dormitory, but here, home. How will I begin, though? How shall I put it? Will I get angry or should I restrain myself and appeal to their sense of reason and duty? Yet inside, he felt neither anger nor rebuke, only pain and disappointment. David Dagan had sons who were a few years older than Edna and they had already done their military service. Maybe instead of going there, he should talk to one of them? But what exactly would he say?

From the time she was a child, Edna had been closer to Nahum than to her mother. Although she rarely expressed this closeness in words, Nahum always knew, from some unspoken mutual understanding, what to ask and what not to ask, when to concede and when to stand his ground. Since her mother's death, Edna had taken it upon herself to drop off her father's clothes at the laundry every Monday and return with a bundle of clean, ironed clothes every Friday; or she would sew on missing buttons for him. Since her brother's death, she came to his apartment every day in the late afternoon, made them coffee and sat with him for an hour or so. They spoke very little, usually just about her studies or his work. Sometimes they talked about a book. They listened to music together. Peeled and ate fruit. After the hour had passed, she would get up, take the cups to the sink but would leave them for her father to wash after she had left for the school dormitory. Though Nahum knew almost nothing about her social life, he did know that her teachers were pleased with her, and he was proud that she'd learned Arabic on her own. A quiet girl, they said about her on the kibbutz, not impetuous like her mother, but devoted and diligent, like her father. What a shame she had cut off her plaits for a short bob with a fringe. With her hair plaited and parted down the middle she had looked just like one of those pioneer girls of an earlier generation.

One evening several months before, Nahum had gone to look for her in her dorm room to bring her a sweater she had left in his apartment. He found her with two of her girlfriends sitting on their beds, all playing recorders, practising a simple scale over and over again. As he came in, he apologised for interrupting them, then laid the folded sweater on the corner of the bed, brushed a speck of invisible dust off the table, apologised again and tip-toed away so as not to disturb them. Outside, he stood under their window in the dark for five minutes and listened: they were now playing a light, lengthy étude that repeated itself in a melancholy way. His heart suddenly clenched. He walked to his apartment, sat down, and listened to the radio until his eyes closed. At night, half awake, he heard the jackals howling close by, as if they were right under his window.

On Tuesday when he came home from work, Nahum showered, got dressed in his ironed khaki trousers and a light-blue shirt, put on the short, shabby coat that gave him the air of a poor intellectual from the previous century, polished his glasses with the corner of his handkerchief and started for the door. Suddenly he remembered the advanced Arabic textbook that Edna had left in his apartment. He wrapped the book very carefully in a plastic bag, tucked it under his arm, put on his grey cap and left the house. Vestiges of rain were still visible in the small puddles and on the fragrant, glistening leaves of the trees. Since he was in no hurry, he took a longer path that meandered past the children's house. He still didn't know what he would say to his daughter or to David Dagan, but he hoped that something would come to him when they were face to face. For a moment he imagined that the whole business between Edna and David Dagan hadn't really happened, but existed only in the malicious imaginations of Roni Shindlin and the other kibbutz gossip-mongers, so that when he finally arrived at David's place he would find him as usual, sitting and drinking an afternoon coffee with some other woman — one of his ex-wives, or Ziva the teacher, or perhaps an entirely new woman. Maybe Edna wouldn't be there at all and he would simply exchange a few words with David at the door, about politics and the government, and he'd decline to stay for coffee and a chess game but instead would say goodbye and go on his way, perhaps to Edna's dorm room where he would find her reading or playing the recorder or doing homework. As always. And he'd return the book to her there.

Walking along, he inhaled the scent of damp earth and the faint smell of fermenting orange peel and cow dung coming from the yard and the barns. He stopped in front of the memorial to the kibbutz's fallen soldiers and saw his son's name there: Yishai Asherov, killed six years ago during the army's incursion into the village of Deir al Nashaf. All eleven names on the memorial were picked out in copper letters and Yishai was the seventh or eighth on the list. Nahum remembered how, as a child, Yishai used to say 'nake' instead of 'snake' and 'ractor' instead of 'tractor'. He reached out and ran his fingertips along the cold copper letters. Then he turned and walked away, still not knowing what he would say, but feeling suddenly dispirited because since his youth he'd had a soft spot in his heart for David Dagan — and even after what had happened, he still felt no anger, only embarrassment and mostly disappointment and sorrow. As he began to walk away from the memorial, the rain started again, not in sheets but in a thin, stubborn drizzle. It wet his cheeks and fogged his glasses, and he thrust the plastic-wrapped book under his worn coat to hold it close to his chest. He seemed to be pressing on his heart as if he didn't feel well. No one passed him on the path, so no one saw his hand pressed against his coat. And perhaps the unlikely relationship between Edna and David Dagan would end of its own accord in a few days? Would she come to her senses and return to her former life? Or would David quickly grow tired of her as he always grew tired of his lovers? She was, after all, a girl who had never before had a boyfriend except, so they said, for a two- or three-week flirtation with Dubi the lifeguard at the swimming pool; while David Dagan was a well-known philanderer.

Nahum Asherov remembered the start of his friendship with David Dagan: during the first few years of the kibbutz, they had been so poor that they lived in tents supplied by the Jewish Agency. Only the five babies lived in the single small house on their land. An ideological debate broke out about who should tend to the babies at night: would only the parents take shifts, or would all the members of the kibbutz? The debate stemmed from a deeper point of contention: did the babies belong, in principle, to their parents or to the entire kibbutz? David Dagan fought for the second position while Nahum Asherov sided with the first. For three nights, the members argued until one o'clock in the morning about whether to decide the question with an open vote or a secret ballot. David Dagan supported the open vote while Nahum Asherov advocated a secret ballot. In the end they agreed to form a committee consisting of David, Nahum and three women who were not yet mothers. The majority of the committee voted that, although the children belonged to the kibbutz, at first the parents would take turns minding the children at night. Although their opinions differed, Nahum secretly admired David Dagan's consistent and unyielding ideological position. David, for his part, respected Nahum's gentleness and patience and was surprised that Nahum, with his quiet persistence, had actually beaten him. When Yishai was killed in the raid on Deir al Nashaf, David Dagan had spent a few nights in Nahum's apartment. This strengthened their long friendship. Sometimes they'd meet in the early evening to play chess and talk about whether or not the kibbutz was living up to its principles.

David Dagan's apartment was located near a stand of cypress trees at the end of a row of houses. He had moved after leaving his fourth wife. Everyone knew that he'd left her because of his relationship with Ziva, a young teacher from the city who stayed on the kibbutz three nights a week. He'd ended things with Ziva when Edna had taken her belongings from the dormitory and moved into his new apartment. Anyone in my shoes, Nahum Asherov thought, would storm in, slap David, grab his daughter and drag her home. Or the opposite: he'd go in quietly and stand in front of them, broken and distraught, as if to say, how could you, aren't you ashamed? Ashamed of what? Nahum asked himself.

And, meanwhile, he lingered a few more minutes in the feeble rain, on the path leading to the door, pressing the book tighter against his chest, the raindrops on his glasses blurring his vision. Distant thunder sounded and it suddenly began to rain harder. Nahum stood under the overhang at the entrance to the apartment and waited. He still had no idea what he would say when David opened the door. And what if Edna answered? David Dagan's neglected front garden was filled with weeds and thistles, dotted with hordes of white snails thanks to the rain. Three pots of withered geraniums stood on the window-sill. Not a sound came from the apartment. Nahum wiped his shoes on the doormat, took a crumpled handkerchief from his pocket and dried his glasses, replaced the handkerchief and knocked twice on the door.

'It's you,' David said warmly, and pulled Nahum inside. 'Wonderful. Come in. Don't stand outside. It's raining. We've been expecting you for a few days now. I was sure you'd come. We have to talk. Edna!' he called out towards the other room, 'make coffee for your father. He's finally here. Take off your coat, Nahum. Sit down. Edna was beginning to think you were angry with us but I told her, you'll see; he'll come. We turned on the heater half an hour ago in your honour. Winter turned up all of a sudden, didn't it? Where did the rain catch you?' He put his large fingers on the sleeve of Nahum's coat and said, 'We really have to talk about this annoying business of all the youngsters just out of the army who now want to skip working and go straight to college. Maybe at our next meeting we should vote about making it mandatory for them to work on the kibbutz for three years before they enroll at college. What do you think, Nahum?'

Nahum, still wearing his cap, said in a flat voice, 'But I don't understand how — '

David interrupted him by putting a wide hand on his shoulder and saying, 'Hear me out; just give me a minute to set things

46

straight. I'm not against higher education, as you know, and I don't object to the younger generation getting academic degrees. On the contrary: someday every barn-worker will have a Ph.D., why not? But never at the expense of the essential work that must be done in the fields and in the animal pens.'

Nahum hesitated. He was still standing in his wet, worn coat, his left arm pressed to his chest to keep the book from slipping. He finally sat down without taking off his coat or cap and without releasing his grip on the book. David Dagan said, 'You probably disagree, don't you, Nahum? Has there ever been a time all these years when you didn't disagree with me? But we've always remained friends.'

Suddenly Nahum hated David Dagan's thick, neatly trimmed moustache with its threads of grey, and his habit of interrupting and asking for just a minute to set things straight. He said, 'But she's your student.'

'Not any more,' David said in an authoritative voice, 'and in a few months, she'll be a soldier. Come here, Edna. Please tell your father that no one has kidnapped you.'

Edna came into the room wearing brown cords and an oversized blue sweater. Her black hair was tied back with a light-coloured ribbon. She carried a tray set with two cups of coffee, a sugar bowl and a small jug of milk. She bent down, put the tray on the table and stood a small distance from the two men, her arms hugging her shoulders as if here, too, she was cold, even though a kerosene heater burned with a clear blue flame. Nahum stole a quick glance at his daughter, then immediately shifted his eyes and blushed as if he had caught a glimpse of her half-naked. She said, 'There are biscuits, too.' Then, after a pause, still standing, she added in her soft, quiet voice, 'Hello, Papa.'

Nahum found neither anger nor rebuke in his heart, only a sharp longing for his daughter, as if she weren't present in the room, three steps away from him, as if she had travelled to a far-off, alien place. He said timidly and with a question mark at the end of his sentence, 'I came to take you home?'

David Dagan put his hand on the nape of Edna's neck, stroked her back, played with her hair a little and said comfortably, 'Edna is not a kettle. She's not something you can just take and put anywhere. Right, Edna?'

She didn't say anything. She stood there next to the heater, her arms hugging her shoulders, ignoring David Dagan's fingers, and stared at the rain on the window.

Nahum looked at her. She seemed quiet

and focused, as if she were thinking about other things. As if she had been distracted from contemplating the choice between these two men, both thirty years older than she. Or as if she had never contemplated the choice in the first place.

They heard the constant sound of the rain beating against the window panes and rushing along the gutters. The heater glowed with a cosy fire. Occasionally they could hear kerosene bubbling through the inner pipes of the heater.

Why did you come here? Nahum asked himself. Did you really think you would slay the dragon and free the abducted princess? You should have stayed at home and waited until she came back. Because, really, all she did was swap a weak father figure for a strong one. And the strong figure will quickly begin to pall. She makes him coffee and takes his laundry in on Monday and returns it on Friday. She'll probably get tired of all that. If only you hadn't been in such a hurry to come here in this rain, if only you'd been smart enough to sit quietly at home and wait for her, sooner or later she'd have come back, either to explain herself or because the love had ended. Love is a kind of infection, possessing then releasing you.

David said, 'Hang on, just give me a

minute to set things straight. You and I, Nahum, have always been connected through friendship despite our disagreements about how to run the kibbutz. And now there is another strong connection between us. That's all. Nothing bad has happened. At the general meeting I plan to propose the idea of three years' mandatory work before college. Obviously you won't support me, but in your heart you know very well that I'm right on this, too. At least don't keep me from mobilising a majority at the meeting. Drink your coffee; it's getting cold.'

Edna said, 'Don't go. Wait till the rain stops, Papa.' Then she said, 'Don't worry about me. I'm fine here.'

Nahum decided not to respond at all. He ignored the coffee his daughter had brought him. He regretted having come. What had he actually wanted? To vanquish love? A fleeting glint of light from the lamp reflected off his glasses. Love suddenly seemed to him to be another of life's obstacles; when you confront it, you have to duck your head and wait until it passes. In another minute David Dagan would probably start a conversation about the government or the advantages of rain. The rare audacity that suffering can sometimes draw from the depths of mild people lent Nahum Asherov's hoarse voice a harsh, bitter tone. 'How could you?'

He shot out of his chair and whipped out the advanced Arabic textbook from his worn coat, intending to slam it on the table hard enough to make the spoons rattle in their cups, but at the last minute he stopped and placed the book down gently as if taking care not to damage it, or the cups, or the oil-cloth-covered table. As he groped his way towards the door, he turned round and saw his daughter standing there watching him with a sad expression, hugging her shoulders, and he saw his good friend sitting with his legs crossed, strong hands encircling a cup, his expression a mixture of compassion, forgiveness and irony. Nahum thrust his head forward and strode towards the door as if he planned to butt it. Instead of slamming it when he went out, he closed it gently, as though afraid of hurting the door or the frame, pulled his cap down almost to his eyes, raised his coat collar and walked along the wet path that led through a pine grove. His glasses instantly beaded with water. He buttoned the top of his coat and pressed his left hand against his chest as if the book were still tucked inside. And, meanwhile, outside it had grown dark.

Father

Sixteen-year-old Moshe Yashar, tall, thin, sad and bespectacled, went to see his teacher David Dagan at the ten-o'clock break and asked his permission to visit his father when school was over and he'd finished work. He planned to stay overnight with relatives in Or Yehuda and get up at four-thirty the next morning to catch the first bus back to the kibbutz so he could be there before school began.

David Dagan patted the boy's shoulder and said warmly, 'These visits to your relatives pull you away from us. And you're almost one of us now.'

Moshe said, 'He's my father.'

David Dagan pondered this for a moment, nodded twice as if agreeing with himself, and asked, 'So tell me, have you learned to swim yet?'

The boy, gazing down at his sandals, said that he could swim a little. His teacher said, 'And stop cutting your hair so short. With that stubble on your head you look like a refugee. It's time you had a decent head of hair like all the other boys.'

After a brief hesitation, he added affectionately, 'All right, go. But only if you come back
tomorrow before the first lesson. And while
you're there, don't forget that you're one of
us now.'

Moshe Yashar was a boarder at our kibbutz.
He was brought to us by a welfare worker: his
mother died when he was seven and when his
father fell ill his uncle Sami from Givat Olga
took in the children. Several years later, when
his uncle also became ill, the Welfare Office
decided to split the children up and send
them to various kibbutzim to live and attend
school. Moshe came to Kibbutz Yekhat at the
beginning of the school year wearing a plain
white shirt without pockets, buttoned all the
way up to the neck, and a black beret. He
quickly learned to walk around barefoot and
dress as we did, in shorts and singlet. We
signed him up for the art club and the current-
events group, and, because he was tall and
agile, he also found his way to the basketball
court. But there was always something of the
outsider about him: when we went on nocturnal forays to the food storeroom to scavenge
treats for a sumptuous midnight feast, he never
came with us. After school, when we all went
to work and then to our parents' house for the
evening, Moshe remained alone in his room,
doing homework, or went to the clubhouse

where, with his glasses sliding down his nose, he would read all the newspapers from beginning to end. And when we lay on the grass at night and sang nostalgic songs under the stars, he was the only one who didn't put his head on the lap of one of the girls. At first we called him an alien and made fun of his shyness, but a few weeks after his arrival we stopped teasing him about his foreignness, which was of a quiet, restrained kind. If someone offended him, Moshe Yashar would look the offender right in the eye. Sometimes he would say in a calm voice, 'You're insulting me.' But he bore no grudges and was always ready to help with any kind of work: carrying, moving, hanging things. He was even willing to help those who'd hurt his feelings, if they asked. After a few months, the 'alien' appellation fell away and the girls began to call him Moshik. There was a unique gentleness in the way he behaved towards the girls, a gentleness in direct contrast to our gruff banter. Moshe spoke to the girls as if there were something marvellous about the mere fact that they were girls.

The school day began at seven in the morning and ended at one, when we had lunch in the school dining room, then went to change into our work clothes. From two until four every day, we worked in the various branches of the kibbutz. Moshe worked in the chicken coop and, unlike many of us, never asked for a different job. He quickly learned to spread feed in the troughs, collect eggs from the shelves that ran the length of the hens' wire cages and arrange them in rows in cartons, set the thermostat in the brooder house and feed the chicks, and he even injected the hens with vaccines. The old-timers who worked in the coop, Shraga Shetchopek and Cheska Honig, were very pleased with him. He was fast and hard-working, quiet and thorough, and he never broke an egg or forgot to spread clean sawdust in the brooder houses where the newly hatched chicks were kept, was never late and never took a sick day or stayed away for any other reason.

David Dagan said to Rivka Rikover, another teacher, 'I let him go to visit his family from after work today till the first lesson tomorrow. Though I'm not completely happy about this trip.'

Rivka said, 'We have to encourage him to break off contact with them. They pull him back.'

David said, 'When we came to this country, we simply left our parents behind. We cut them out of our lives at a stroke and that was that.'

Rivka said, 'That boy has excellent

qualities: he's quiet, hard-working, and he gets on with people.'

David said, 'On the whole, I have a very optimistic view of the Sephardim. We'll have to invest a great deal in them, but the investment will pay off. In another generation or two, they'll be just like us.'

After David Dagan gave him permission to go, Moshe hurried to the room he shared with Tamir and Dror. By the end of the ten o'clock break, he had finished packing his small bag with underwear, socks, a spare shirt, his toothbrush and toothpaste, a copy of *The Plague* by Albert Camus, and his old black beret, which he kept hidden under a pile of clothes in the left compartment of the wardrobe under Tamir's.

After break they had a history lesson. David Dagan, their teacher, gave a lecture on the French Revolution, dwelling on Karl Marx's view of it: as a foreshadowing and early stage of the necessary and inevitable historical revolutions that would culminate in a classless society. Gideon, Lilah and Carmela raised their hands and asked questions that David Dagan answered firmly and at length: 'Just give me just a minute,' he said, 'so we can set things straight.'

Moshe cleaned his glasses and wrote everything down in his notebook — he was a conscientious student — but refrained from asking questions. Some weeks earlier, he'd read several chapters of *Das Kapital* in the school library and he didn't like Karl Marx: he felt that there could have been an exclamation mark after almost every sentence, and that put him off. Marx claimed, so it seemed to Moshe, that economic, social and historical laws were as clear and immutable as the laws of nature. And Moshe had his doubts even about the immutability of the laws of nature.

When Lilah remarked that in order to have progress, there have to be victims, David Dagan agreed with her and added that history is by no means a garden party. Bloodshed repelled Moshe and garden parties did not particularly appeal to him either. Not that he'd ever been to a garden party, but neither did he think he'd ever want to attend one. He spent his free time reading in the empty library when his classmates were with their parents. Among the books he read was a translated World War II story of escape and survival in the frozen north, entitled *We Die Alone* by David Howarth. His reading was leading him to the simple conclusion that most people need more affection than they can find. These were the thoughts that filled his mind during the lesson on the French

Revolution. After history class two lessons remained, trigonometry and agriculture, and when they were over we all dashed out of class straight to our rooms to put on our work clothes and race off to the dining room for a quick lunch.

Lunch consisted of spinach patties with mashed potatoes, sour pickles and cooked carrots. We were hungry, so we also wolfed down bread and asked for more mashed potatoes. There was a large tin jug of cold water on every table, and we each drank two or three glasses because of the heat. Flies buzzed around our heads and large dusty ceiling fans whirred above us. Dessert was stewed fruit. When we finished eating, we took our dishes and silverware to the hatch that opened into the dishwashing room and went off to our jobs: Tamir to the garage, Dror to the fodder fields, Carmela to the baby house and Lilah to the laundry.

Moshe, wearing his dusty work clothes and shoes that stank of chicken droppings, crossed the road of cypress trees, passed two abandoned sheds and a tin-roofed lean-to and reached the large chicken coop. Even from a distance, the smell of the coop enveloped him: the stench of chicken excrement, of the dust that rises from the feed, of torn-out feathers that stuck to the wire netting, along

61

with another vague smell of overcrowding and suffocation. Cheska Honig was waiting for him, sitting on a small stool sorting eggs into cartons according to size. Moshe asked her how she was, then told her that today, right after work, he was taking the four-o'clock bus to visit his father. Cheska pointed out that when she was young, she just got up one day and ran away from home to go to Eretz Israel and join a kibbutz, so she actually never said goodbye to her parents. The Nazis murdered them in Lithuania. 'Where is this family of yours, anyway?' Cheska asked Moshe. 'They live in some kind of immigrants' camp?'

In a low, even voice Moshe told her what he told everyone here who asked him, that his mother died and his father fell ill and his uncle fell ill too, so he and his brothers and sisters were sent to live in various kibbutzim. As they spoke, he rolled the feed cart under the large funnel of the feed container and filled it to the brim. He pushed it along the concrete walk between the two rows of cages and began to fill the troughs with feed. Under the cages crammed with chickens were piles of droppings. When here and there he found a dead chicken in a cage, he opened the cage, took out the carcass and placed it gently on the concrete walk behind him. When he finished distributing the feed into all the troughs, he went back to collect the carcasses. Low moaning filled the air as if the hens, squeezed together two-by-two in the cages, were keening a faint, persistent, lost lament. Only now and then did a sharp screech of fear burst from one of the cages, as if a chicken had suddenly guessed how all of this would end. After all, no two chickens are or ever have been exactly alike. They all look the same to us, but they are actually different from one another the same way that people are, and since the creation of the world, no two identical creatures have ever been born. Moshe had already decided to become a vegetarian one day, maybe even a vegan, but had postponed implementing the decision because being a vegan among the kibbutz boys would not be easy. Even without being a vegetarian, he had to work hard day and night to seem like everyone else here. He had to keep his feelings to himself. Pretend. He thought of the cruelty of eating meat and of the fate of these hens, doomed to spend their entire lives packed tightly in wire cages, unable to move even one step. Someday, Moshe thought, a future generation will call us murderers, unable to comprehend how we could eat the flesh of creatures like ourselves, rob them of the feel of the earth and the smell of the grass, hatch them in automatic incubators, raise them in crowded cages, force-feed them, steal all their eggs before they hatch, and finally, slit their throats, pluck their feathers, tear them limb from limb, gorge ourselves on them and drool and lick the fat from our lips. For months now Moshe had been plotting to open a cage and surreptitiously steal a chicken, only one, hide it under his shirt, away from the watchful eyes of Cheska and Shraga, spirit it out of the coop and set it free on the other side of the kibbutz fence. But what would an abandoned chicken do all alone in the fields? At night the jackals would come and tear it to pieces.

He was suddenly disgusted with himself, a feeling he had often and for many and sundry reasons. Then he was disgusted by his disgust, scornfully calling himself a bleeding heart, a label that David Dagan sometimes applied to those who recoiled from the necessary cruelty of the revolution. Moshe respected David Dagan, a man of principle with strong opinions who spread a fatherly wing over him and all the other students in their school. It was David Dagan who had welcomed him into Kibbutz Yekhat and guided him gently but firmly into his new life. He was the one who signed Moshe up for the art club and the current-events group, and he it was who defended him fiercely against the other children's mocking attitude when he first arrived. Moshe knew, as we all did, that David was living with a very young girl, Edna Asherov, Nahum the electrician's daughter. There had been many women in David's life, and though that surprised Moshe, he said to himself that, after all, David Dagan wasn't an ordinary person like the rest of us, but a philosopher. He didn't judge David because he didn't like to judge other people and because he was so grateful to him. But he did wonder. He had often tried to put himself in David Dagan's shoes, but he was never able to imagine the teacher's easy sense of entitlement when it came to women and girls. No just social revolution, he thought, not even the final, cruel one that David spoke about, could lead to equality between people like David, who attracted women effortlessly, and people like me, who would never dare, not even in their imaginations.

Yes, Moshe Yashar did occasionally dream of his classmate Carmela Nevo's shy smile and of her fingers playing melancholy songs on the recorder, but he never dared to approach her, not with words, and almost never with looks. From where he sat in class, two rows behind her, he could see the curve of her slender neck as she bent over her notebook and the soft down of the hair on her nape. Once, when Carmela was standing between the light and the wall talking to one of the girls, he walked past and stroked her shadow. Afterwards he lay awake half the night, unable to sleep.

Cheska said, 'After you've set the thermostat in the brooder house and checked that there's water in the trough and fed the chicks and put all the egg cartons in the refrigerator, you can go. I'll write down the daily summary for you today. And I'll let you go fifteen minutes early so you have time to shower and change and catch the four-o'clock bus.'

Moshe, who was collecting the dead chickens he had left on the walkway to drop them outside in the barrel to be burned, said, 'Thank you.' And added, 'I'll be back tomorrow morning and I'll come to work fifteen minutes early in the afternoon.'

Cheska said, 'The main thing is that you show them there that you are a total kibbutznik now.'

Alone in the shower, he scrubbed off the smells of the coop with soap and water, dried himself and put on long ironed trousers and a white Sabbath shirt, rolling the sleeves up past his elbows. He went to his room, took the bag he had packed during the ten-o'clock break and left quickly, cutting across the lawn and past the flower beds. Zvi Provizor, the gardener, was kneeling at one of them, pulling up weeds. He looked up and asked Moshe where he was off to. Moshe was going to say that he was on his way to visit his father in the hospital but instead he said only, 'Town.'

Zvi Provizor asked, 'Why? What do they have there that we don't have here?'

Moshe said nothing, but thought about replying: 'Strangers.'

* * *

At the central bus station, when he got off the Kibbutz Yekhat bus and boarded the one to the hospital, Moshe chose to sit in the last row of seats. He took his threadbare black beret out of his bag and put it on his head, pulling it down so that it hid half his forehead. He buttoned his shirt all the way up and rolled his sleeves all the way down to his wrists. And instantly looked as he had on the day the welfare worker brought him to Kibbutz Yekhat. He was still wearing the summer sandals they'd given him on the kibbutz, but he was almost sure his father wouldn't notice them. There were very few things his father still noticed. The bus wove through the alleyways near the central bus station and the smell of heavily fried food and combusted

67

petrol drifted in through the open windows. Moshe thought about the girls in his class who had begun to call him Moshik. Now that the teasing and mocking had passed, Moshe found that he was enjoying kibbutz social life. He liked school, where he could sit in class barefoot on summer days and argue freely with his teachers without having to show any of the usual subservience. He liked the basketball court. He also liked the art club and the current-events group meetings in the evenings where they discussed adult matters, and where Israeli life was usually represented by two camps: the progressive and the old-world. Moshe was well aware that part of him still belonged to the old world because he didn't always accept progressive ideas, but rather than argue, he simply listened. He spent his free time reading the books by Dostoevsky, Camus and Kafka that he borrowed from the library, finding himself deeply touched by the enigmas contained in their pages. He was drawn more to unsolved questions than to glib solutions. But he told himself that perhaps this was still part of the adjustment process and in a few months he'd learn to see the world the way David Dagan and the other teachers wanted their students to see it. How good it was to be one of them. Moshe envied the boys who rested their heads so easily on the girls' laps as they lay on the large lawn in the evening and sang work songs and patriotic tunes. Until the age of twelve, so he was told, girls and boys had showered naked together. Chills of excitement and fear had run down his back when he heard that. Day after day, Tamir and Dror and the other boys had seen Carmela Nevo naked, and they grew inured to what they saw, while for him, even the thought of the curve of her neck and the soft down on the nape made him tremble with longing and shame. Would he become one of them someday? He yearned for that day but was afraid of it too, and he also knew in his heart of hearts that it would never come.

★　★　★

The bus had already left Tel Aviv and was driving jerkily from town to town, pulling up at every stop, letting passengers on and off, hard-working people who spoke Romanian, Arabic, Yiddish, Hungarian, some carrying live chickens or large bundles wrapped in tattered blankets or old suitcases tied with ropes. When shouting and pushing occasionally broke out on the bus, the driver rebuked the passengers and they cursed him. At one point, the driver stopped on the side of the road between two small villages, got off, stood with his back to the bus and urinated in a field. When he boarded again and started the engine, a murky cloud of stinking diesel fuel filled the air. It was hot and humid, and the passengers were bathed in sweat. The trip was very long, even longer than the ride from Kibbutz Yekhat to Tel Aviv because the bus circled through the small towns and an immigrant camp. Citrus groves and fields of thorns filled the unpopulated areas. Dusty cypress or eucalyptus trees with peeling bark lined the sides of the road. Finally, when day began to soften into evening, Moshe stood up, pulled the cord to stop the bus and stepped off onto the fork in the dirt road that led to the hospital.

The moment he got off the bus, Moshe saw a small mongrel puppy, grey-brown with white patches on its head. It was running diagonally through the bushes towards the road, which it crossed just as the bus began to move. The front tyre missed it, but the back one crushed the creature before it even had a chance to bark. There was only a light thump and the bus continued on its way. The little dog's body lay on the cracked road, still twitching violently, raising its head again and again and banging it on the hard asphalt each time it fell back. Its legs flailed in the air and a stream of dark blood spurted from the open jaw past the small, shiny teeth, and another trickle of blood oozed from its hind quarters. Moshe ran over, kneeled on the road and held the dog's head gently until it stopped twitching and its eyes glazed over. Then he picked up the small, still-warm body so that no other cars would run over it and carried it in his arms to the foot of a eucalyptus tree with a whitewashed trunk near the bus stop and laid it down. He cleaned his hands with some dirt but couldn't wipe the bloodstains off his trousers and white Sabbath shirt. He knew his father was not likely to notice it. There were very few things his father still noticed. Moshe stood there for a moment, took out a handkerchief and wiped the moisture off his glasses; then, since night was falling, he began to walk quickly, almost running along the dirt road.

The hospital, a twenty-minute walk from the road, was surrounded by a wall of untreated breeze blocks topped with barbed wire. By the time he reached it the blood on his clothes had congealed into rust-coloured stains.

A fat, sweaty guard wearing a yarmulke stood at the hospital gate, blocking the entrance with his thick body. He told Moshe that visiting hours were over a long time ago

and he should 'go and come back tomorrow'.
Moshe, his eyes still filled with tears for the
dead dog, tried to explain that he'd come all
the way from Kibbutz Yekhat to see his father,
and he had to be back at school on the
kibbutz by seven o'clock tomorrow morning.
The fat guard, who was in a jovial mood,
pointed to the black beret on Moshe's head
and said, 'They don't keep the Sabbath on
the kibbutz and they eat *treyf* there, don't
they?' Moshe tried to explain, but the tears
choked him. The guard softened and said,
'Don't cry, son, go in, it's okay, go in, but
next time come between four and five, not at
night. And don't stay more than half an hour.'
Moshe thanked him and for some reason
reached out to shake the guard's hand. The
guard didn't take the proffered hand, but
tapped the black beret on the young boy's
head twice and said, 'Just make sure you keep
the Sabbath.'

Moshe crossed a small, neglected garden
with two benches badly in need of fresh paint
and walked through the iron-barred door that
opened when he rang a raspy bell. In the
entrance hall some ten men and women were
sitting on metal chairs that lined the walls,
which were painted a sort of khaki colour to
halfway up. The men and women were all
wearing striped hospital gowns and flat

slippers. Some were speaking to each other in hesitant voices. The supervisor, a strapping fellow wearing a loud flowered shirt and army-issue trousers and boots was standing in a corner of the room chewing gum. An older woman was knitting furiously, though she had neither needles nor wool. Her lips moved in a low mutter. A spindly, stoop-shouldered man stood with his back to the room, clutching the bars of the window and speaking to the now darkening world outside. An old woman was sitting alone near the door, sucking hard on her thumb and mumbling prayers of supplication. His father was out on the balcony, which was covered from top to bottom with netting. He was sitting on a grey metal chair next to a small metal table, also grey, with a tin mug of tea cooling on it. Moshe sat down in a metal chair beside him and said, 'Hello, Father.' He sat hunched over so that his father wouldn't see the bloodstains on his clothes.

The father said hello without looking at his son.

'I've come to see you.'

The father nodded and said nothing.

'I've come by bus.'

The father asked, 'Where did he go?'

'Who?'

'Moshe.'

'I'm Moshe.'

'You're Moshe.'

'I'm Moshe. I've come to visit you.'

'You're Moshe.'

'How are you, Father?'

The father asked again, with concern and profound sadness, in a voice trembling with pain, 'Where did he go? Where?'

Moshe took his wrinkled, veiny hand, worn out by hard work building roads and planting crops, and said, 'I've come from the kibbutz, Father. I've come from Kibbutz Yekhat. I've come to visit you. Everything is fine with me. It's going very well.'

'You're Moshe.'

So Moshe began to tell his father about his school. About his teacher, David Dagan. About the library. About working in the chicken coop. About the girls who sing beautiful, nostalgic songs. Then he opened his shoulder bag and took out *The Plague*, with its green cover, and read the first two paragraphs to his father. His father, a yarmulke on his slightly tilted head, listened attentively, weary eyes half closed, then suddenly picked up the tin mug, looked at the now-cool tea, shook his head sadly, put the mug down again and asked, 'Where did he go?'

Moshe said, 'I'll go to the kitchen and get you a fresh cup of tea. Hot tea.'

His father wiped his forehead with his hand and, as if awakening from sleep, said again, 'You're Moshe.'

Moshe held his father's hand and didn't hug him, but kept pressing the limp, brown hand. He told his father about the basketball court, the books he'd read, the debates in the current-events group and his participation in the discussions in the art club, about Joseph K. from Kafka's book, and about David Dagan, who'd already had several wives and lovers and now lived with a seventeen-year-old girl, but always gave his full attention to his students and had defended him fiercely when the others teased and mocked him during his first few weeks on the kibbutz. David Dagan, he has a habit of saying to people, 'Just give me a minute so we can set things straight.' Moshe spoke to his father for about ten minutes, and his father closed his eyes, then opened them and said sorrowfully, 'All right. You can go now. You're Moshe?'

Moshe said, 'Yes, Father,' and added, 'Don't worry, Father. I'll come to see you again in two weeks. They let me come. David Dagan lets me come.'

The father nodded and dropped his chin to his chest, as if in mourning.

Moshe said, 'Goodbye, Father.' Then he said, 'I'll see you soon. Don't worry.'

From the door he gave a last look at his father, who was sitting utterly still staring at the tin mug. On the way out Moshe asked the supervisor in the army trousers, 'How is he?'

The supervisor said, 'He's fine. Quiet.' Then he said, 'I wish they were all like him,' and finally added, 'You're a very good son. Bless you.'

★ ★ ★

When he left it was almost dark outside. Moshe was suddenly filled with that familiar sense of self-loathing. He took his black beret off and put it in his bag. He rolled his sleeves up to his biceps again and undid his top button. Only thorns and couch grass grew in the small front garden of the hospital. But someone had forgotten a dish towel on the bench and someone had lost the belt to his robe among the thorns. Moshe noticed those details because he was drawn to details. He thought about Cheska Honig, who had taught him to keep an eye out for sick hens and isolate them before they infected the whole coop. And he thought about his class-mates lying on one of the lawns now, the boys' heads resting on the girls' laps as they sang nostalgic songs. One of them, Tamir or Dror or Gideon or Arnon, was now putting

76

his blond head on Carmela Nevo's lap, its heat caressing his cheek. Moshe would give everything he had to be there now. Once and for all to be one of them. And yet he knew very well that it would never happen. As he walked through the gate the jovial guard asked, 'What's this, you go in with a hat on and come out without it?'

Moshe said only goodnight and turned onto the dirt path that led from the hospital to the road. It was dark and empty. Not a single car drove past. Pinpoints of light shone in the distance and he could hear the braying of a donkey. The faint voices of children also came from the direction of the lights. He kneeled on the ground and sat back on his legs at the foot of the whitewashed eucalyptus tree, close to where he had laid the run-over dog, and waited. He waited for a long time. He thought he could hear sounds of jagged weeping coming from the hospital, but he wasn't sure. He sat there motionless, and listened.

Little Boy

Leah, his wife, had gone off to attend a ten-day course at the Kibbutzim College of Education that would train her to be a childminder in the children's house. Roni Shindlin was happy to have a few days without her. He showered after his shift in the metalwork shop and at four in the afternoon went to the children's house to pick up his five-year-old son Oded. On the days it wasn't raining, he held Oded's small hand and they went for a stroll around the kibbutz. Oded wore green boots, flannel trousers, a sweater and a jacket. Roni always tied the strings of the boy's hat under his chin because his ears were sensitive to the cold. Then he picked him up, hugged him and took him to see the cows and the sheep. Oded was afraid of the cows, which wallowed in wet dung and mooed faintly from time to time. His father recited for him: 'I never saw a purple cow/I never hope to see one/But I can tell you anyhow/I'd rather see than be one.'

Oded asked, 'Why is it roaring?'

Roni explained, 'Cows don't roar. Cows moo. Lions roar.'

'Why do lions roar?'

'They're calling their friends.'

'Their friends are mean.'

'Their friends play with them.'

'They're mean.'

Oded was a short little boy, slow and always frightened. He was often sick: he had diarrhoea almost every week and in winter he had ear infections. The children in his kindergarten tormented him constantly. He spent most of the day sitting alone on a mat in a corner, his thumb in his mouth, his back to the room and his face to the wall, playing with wooden blocks or a rubber duck that squealed mournfully when you squeezed it, and he squeezed it all the time. He'd had it since he was a year old. The children called him Oded-pees-his-bed and when the child-minder turned her back they pulled his hair. He cried softly for hours, snot running down to his mouth and chin. The childminders didn't like him either because he didn't know how to stand up for himself, or because he wouldn't play with the others and he cried so much. At the breakfast table he would pick at his porridge and leave most of it in the bowl. When they scolded him he cried. When they tried to coax him into eating he withdrew into himself and was silent. Five years old and he still wet his bed every night, so the childminders had to spread a rubber sheet under the regular one. He got up wet every morning and the children made fun of him. He would sit barefoot in his wet pajamas on his wet bed, his thumb in his mouth, and, instead of trying to change into dry clothes, he'd cry quietly, the snot mingling with his tears and smearing his cheeks, until the childminder arrived and scolded him, 'Oh really, get dressed, Oded. Wipe your nose. Enough crying. Stop being such a baby.'

The Committee for Preschoolers instructed Leah, his mother, to be firm with him in order to wean him off this self-indulgent behaviour. And so, during the afternoons he spent at his parents' house, Leah saw to it that he sat with his back straight, always finished everything on his plate and never sucked his thumb. If he cried, she punished him for being a crybaby. She was against hugging and kissing, believing that the children of our new society had to be strong and resilient. She thought Oded's problems stemmed from the fact that his teachers and childminders let him get away with things he shouldn't and forgave him his oddities. Roni, for his part, hugged and kissed Oded only when Leah wasn't around. When she was gone, he'd take a bar of chocolate out of his pocket and break off two or three squares for Oded. Father and son kept those squares of chocolate a secret from Leah and everyone else. More than once, Roni had intended to take issue with Leah about how she treated their son, but he feared her angry outbursts, which drove Oded to crawl under the bed with his duck and cry soundlessly until his mother's anger subsided — and even then the boy was in no hurry to leave his hiding place.

On the kibbutz, Roni Shindlin was considered a gossip and a comedian, but in his own home, he hardly ever joked because Leah couldn't stand his wisecracks, which she found coarse and tasteless. Both Leah and Roni chainsmoked the cheap Silon cigarettes the kibbutz distributed to its members, and their small apartment was always full of smoke. The smell persisted even at night because it had been absorbed by the furniture and the walls and hovered under the ceiling. Leah didn't like unnecessary touching and talking. She believed in solid principles. She adhered to all the kibbutz tenets with a zealot's fervour. In her view, a couple on the kibbutz should live a simple life.

Their apartment was furnished with a plywood bookcase and a sofa with a foam rubber mattress that opened into a double bed at night and was closed again every morning. There were also a coffee table, two wicker armchairs, an upholstered armchair and a rough floor mat. A painting of a field of sunflowers glowing in the sun hung on the wall, and a mortar-shell casing that served as a vase for a bouquet of dry thorns stood in the corner of the room. And, of course, the air reeked of cigarettes.

In the evening, after the work schedule for the next day had been hung on the bulletin board, Roni liked to sit with his friends and acquaintances at his regular table at the far end of the dining hall, smoking and talking about the goings-on in the kibbutz members' lives. Nothing escaped his notice. Other people's lives aroused his unflagging curiosity and unleashed a torrent of witticisms. He thought that the higher our ideals, the more absurd our weaknesses and contradictions. Sometimes, with a smile, he quoted Levi Eshkol, who said that a person is only human, and even that only rarely. He would light himself a fresh cigarette and say to his cronies in a slightly nasal voice, 'Some people play musical chairs, but here, we play musical mates. First Boaz ups and leaves Osnat for Ariella Barash and now Ariella ups and leaves Boaz for her cat and tomorrow some newly abandoned woman will come and collect the newly abandoned Boaz. In the words of the Bible: 'I have not seen the righteous forsaken or his children begging for . . . a warm bed.'

Or he'd say, 'Anyone on Kibbutz Yekhat who needs a wife can just stand in line at the bottom of David Dagan's steps and wait for a little while. Women are flicked out of there like cigarette butts.'

Roni Shindlin and his tablemates sometimes laughed raucously, and the kibbutz members did their best not to become the butt of their jokes.

At ten at night, Roni and his gang dispersed to their apartments, and he would stop in at the children's house to check on Oded and tuck him in. Then he'd trudge home, sit down on the steps to take off his shoes so as not to track in the mud, and tiptoe inside in his stocking feet. Leah would be sitting there, chainsmoking, listening to the radio. She listened to the radio every night. Roni would also light up, his last cigarette of the day, and sit down across from her without speaking. At ten-thirty they put out their cigarettes, turned off the light and went to sleep, he wrapped in his blanket and she in hers, because they had to get up before six in the morning for work.

In the metalwork shop Roni was known to be a hard worker devoted to his job, and he also never missed a meeting of the Farm Management Committee, where he was always on the side of those who supported careful, balanced management of the agricultural divisions and opposed potentially reckless initiatives. He voted for a limited expansion of the chicken coop but against taking bank loans.

He had a stamp collection that he pored over with Oded every day after work: they would sit with their heads bent, almost touching, over the coffee table, the room warmed by a kerosene heater that burned with a blue flame. With water from a small bowl, Oded would wet the pieces of envelopes that bore the stamps in order to melt the glue and separate them from the paper. Then, under his father's supervision, he'd place the stamps face down on a piece of blotting paper to dry. As Roni arranged the stamps in an album, following the English catalogue, he would explain to Oded about Japan, the land of the rising sun, about the freezing country called Iceland, about Aden and the ancient *Hazarmaveth*, the Courtyard of Death, near the Strait of Tears, about Panama and the large canal that had been dug through it.

Leah squeezed fresh orange juice for them, admonishing Oded to drink it all, then she sat down in her corner and read an education journal. Every now and then they heard a faint burbling from the pipes of the kerosene heater, and the flame behind the iron grate flared up momentarily. Outside, the rain and wind pounded the closed shutters and the branch of a ficus tree brushed against the outer wall again and again as if begging for mercy. Roni stood up, emptied the ashtray and rinsed it under the tap. Oded sucked his thumb and clung to his father. Leah scolded him, 'Stop sucking. And you, stop spoiling him. He's spoiled enough as it is.' Then she added, 'He's better off eating an orange instead, and he should get rid of that pathetic duck of his. Boys don't play with dolls.'

Now that Leah had gone away for ten days, Roni went to the children's house every afternoon at four o'clock to pick up Oded and his squealing duck. With the boy astride his shoulders, he'd stroll around the cow barns and chicken coops. The acrid smell of rotting orange peel rose from the fermentation pit, mingling with the heavy stench of animal feed and wet manure from the barn. A damp wind blew in from the west and an early twilight fell on the storerooms and sheds and enveloped our small, red-roofed houses. Now and then a bird chirped piercingly in a treetop and the sheep in their pen replied with a heartbreaking bleat. Sometimes it began to drizzle and father and son hunched over and hurried home.

At home after their stroll, Roni coaxed Oded into eating a slice of bread and jam and drinking a cup of cocoa. Oded reluctantly nibbled two or three bites of bread, took a sip of the cocoa and said, 'No more, Daddy. Now stamps.'

After Roni had cleared the table and put the dishes in the sink, he took down the green album and the two of them bent over it, heads almost touching. Roni lit a cigarette and explained to Oded that stamps are small visitors from distant countries, and each visitor is here to tell us a story about its homeland, its countryside and famous people, its holidays and beautiful buildings. Oded asked if there were countries where children are allowed to sleep with their parents at night and where children aren't mean and don't hit. Roni didn't know how to answer, so he just said that there are good people and cruel people everywhere, and explained the word 'cruel' to Oded. In his heart, Roni believed that here cruelty is sometimes disguised as self-righteousness or dedication to principles, and he knew that no one was completely free of it. Not even he himself.

Oded grew anxious as seven-thirty approached, the hour he had to go back to the children's house and leave his father for the night. He didn't plead to stay at home, but instead went to the toilet to pee, and when he didn't come out Roni had to go in after him and found him sitting on the closed toilet, sucking his thumb and hugging his rubber duck, its once-red bill now faded and one of its eyes slightly sunken into its head.

Roni said, 'Dedi. We have to go. It's late.'

Oded said, 'We can't, we just can't. There's a big wolf in the woods we have to pass on the way.'

Finally they both put on their coats. Roni helped Oded into his green boots and tied the strings of his hat under his chin. He took a large, thick stick from behind the steps for chasing away the wolf, held Oded in his arms and walked to the children's house. The boy hugged his father's head with one hand, and in the other he held the duck so tightly that it emitted a constant stream of faint squeals. When they passed the grove behind the dining hall, Roni waved his stick, striking the wet air every which way until the wolf ran off. Oded thought about that for a moment, then said sadly that the wolf would come back late at night when the parents were asleep. Roni promised that the night guard would chase away the wolf, but the boy was inconsolable because he knew very well that the wolf would devour the night guard.

When they reached the children's house,

the electric heater was already on in the dining room and there were plates on the small tables, each filled with a slice of bread and yellow cheese, half a hardboiled egg, tomato slices, four olives and a small mound of cream cheese. The childminder, Hemda, a dumpy woman wearing a white apron around her waist, made sure that the children placed their boots in a neat row by the door and hung their coats on the wall hooks above their boots. Then the parents went outside to smoke, the children ate and took their plates and cups to the sink and the monitors wiped the tables.

After the meal the parents were allowed to go in and put their children to bed. The children, in flannel pyjamas, gathered around the sinks, screamed and pushed each other, washed their faces and brushed their teeth and climbed noisily into bed. The parents were given ten minutes to read them a story or sing them a lullaby, then they said good-night and left. Hemda turned off the lights, except for a small one in the dining room. She stayed for several more minutes, forbade the children to whisper, ordered them to go to sleep, gave them another warning, said good-night, leaving a pale light on in the shower room, turned off the electric heater and left.

The children waited until she was gone, then got out of bed barefoot and began to run around the bedrooms and the dining room. They hurled their muddy boots at each other, growing rowdier by the minute. The boys wrapped blankets round their heads and frightened the girls by roaring, 'We're Arabs, we're attacking now.' The shrieking girls huddled together, and one of them, Atida, filled a bottle with water and sprayed the Arabs. The mayhem didn't end until Eviatar, a broad-shouldered boy, suggested, 'Hey, let's go and snatch Oded's duck.'

Oded hadn't got out of bed when the others did but instead lay with his face to the wall and thought about a country from the stamp collection that his father said was called the *Hazarmaveth,* the Courtyard of Death. The name frightened him and he thought that the courtyard of the children's house located in the darkness right on the other side of the wall was also a *hazarmaveth.* He pulled the blanket over his head and hugged the rubber duck, knowing it was dangerous to fall asleep or to cry. He waited for the others to get tired and go back to bed, hoping they'd forget about him tonight. His mother was away, his father had gone to smoke with his friends at their table in the dining hall, the childminder, Hemda, was off somewhere and the *Hazarmaveth* was right there in the darkness behind the thin wall, the door wasn't locked and there was a wolf lurking in the woods they had to pass on the way home.

Tadmor, Tamir and Rina tore off his blanket and threw it on the floor, and Dalit chanted in an infuriating singsong: 'Oded-pees-his-bed is out of his head.'

Eviatar said, 'Now he'll cry.' And he said in an oh-so-sweet voice to Oded, 'So cry a little for us, Oded. Just a little. We're all asking you nicely.'

Oded curled into himself, brought his knees up to his stomach, dropped his head down between his shoulders and clutched his duck, which squealed weakly.

'His duck is filthy.'

'Let's wash the duck.'

'Let's wash his peepee. His peepee's filthy too.'

'Give us the duck, Oded-pees-his-bed. Come on, give it to us. Be nice.'

Eviatar tried to pull the duck from Oded's grasp, but the boy held on to it with all his might, pressing it hard against his stomach. Tadmor and Tamir pulled at Oded's arms and he kicked them with his bare feet, and Rina pulled at his pajamas. Tadmor and Tamir pried his fingers away from the duck and Eviatar wrapped his hand around it, wrenched it away from Oded and waved it in the air, dancing on one leg, chanting, 'Oded's dirty duck is out of luck. Whattya say, let's chuck it away!'

Oded gritted his teeth, fighting not to cry, but his eyes welled and snot ran from his nose onto his mouth and chin. He got out of bed barefoot and tried to attack Eviatar, who was a lot taller and stronger. Eviatar pretended to be afraid and waved the duck high over Oded's head, passing it straight to Tamir, who passed it to Rina, who passed it to Tadmor. Oded, suddenly filled with the despair and fury of the weak, gathered momentum and charged Eviatar as hard as he could, smashing into his stomach and almost knocking him down. The girls, Dalit and Rina, squealed with delight. Eviatar straightened up, pushed Oded away and punched him hard in the nose. When Oded was finally lying on the floor sobbing, Dalit said, 'Let's get him some water,' and Tadmor said, 'Stop it. That's enough. What's wrong with you? Leave him alone.' But Eviatar went to the dining room, took a pair of scissors out of the drawer, cut off the rubber duck's head and went back to the bedroom, the duck's body in his right hand, its head in his left. He bent over Oded, who was still lying on the floor, and laughed. 'Choose, Oded,' he said. 'You can choose.'

Oded got to his feet, pushed his way through the children crowded around him, ran blindly to the door, opened it and bolted straight out into the darkness of the *Hazarmaveth* that lay beyond the children's house. He ran barefoot in the mud, shaking all over in his pyjamas from cold and fear, ran and hopped, like a hunted rabbit, completely soaked by the rain that dripped from his hair down his cheeks and mixed with his tears; he passed blocks of dark buildings, crossed through the darkness of the small grove near the dining hall, heard the thudding of the black wolf's paws pursuing him, felt its breath on the back of his neck, ran faster as the rain grew stronger, the wind beat against his face, and he stumbled and fell onto his knees in a puddle, stood up wet and covered in mud and ran on alone in the darkness between one streetlamp and the next, ran and wept in small, rapid sobs, ran, his ears frozen and stinging, ran until he reached his parents' house where he dropped onto the steps, afraid to go inside, afraid they'd be angry with him and return him to the children's house; and there, on the steps, his little body curled up and frozen and shaking, his father found him crying soundlessly when he came back from the evening's gossip session in the dining hall.

Roni took his son in his arms, carried him inside, removed the wet pajamas and cleaned off the mud and mucus with a washcloth, then rubbed his frozen body with a large, coarse towel to warm him. He swathed the boy in a warm blanket and turned on the heater while Oded recounted what had happened in the children's house. Roni told him to wait beside the heater and bolted out into the rain, running, panting, burning with rage, as he raced wildly up the hill.

When he reached the children's house, his shoes heavy with mud, he saw the night guard, Berta Brom, who tried to tell him something, but he didn't hear and didn't want to hear. Blind and deaf with despair and fury, he burst into Oded's room, turned on the light, bent over and yanked a gentle, quiet boy named Yair from under his blanket, stood him on his bed and slapped his face savagely over and over again until the boy's nose began to bleed and his head banged against the wall with the force of the blows, as Roni shouted in a rasping voice, 'This is nothing! Nothing! I will kill anyone who touches Oded again!'

Berta, the night guard in the children's house, grabbed him by the shoulders and pulled him off the child, who flopped onto the bed, his sobs thin and piercing, and said, 'You've gone crazy, Roni, completely crazy.' Roni punched her in the chest, then ran outside and dashed through the mud and rain back to his son.

Father and son slept with their arms around each other all night on the sofa that opened into a double bed, and in the morning they stayed in the apartment. Roni didn't go to work and he didn't take Oded to the children's house, he just spread jam on a slice of bread and warmed a cup of cocoa. At eight-thirty in the morning, Yoav, the kibbutz secretary, appeared grim-faced at the door and curtly informed Roni that he was expected in the kibbutz office at exactly five o'clock tomorrow afternoon for a personal interview at a joint meeting of the Social and Pre-school Education Committees.

At lunch, Roni's friends sat at the gossip table without him and talked about what the entire kibbutz had been talking about since morning. They speculated about what Roni would say if someone else had done those things. You can never know, they said, such a quiet guy with a sense of humour, and look at what he's capable of. At three in the afternoon, Leah appeared, having been summoned by phone from her course. Before going home, she stopped at the children's house and left warm underwear, clean clothes and boots for the boy. Tight-lipped, a cigarette burning between her fingers, she informed Roni that after what happened, she and she alone will be in charge of Oded and, what's more, she has decided that, for the boy's own good, he will return to the children's house that night.

The rain had stopped, but the sky was still heavy with low clouds and a cold, damp wind had been gusting in from the west all day. The room filled with a cloud of cigarette smoke. At seven-thirty in the evening Leah bundled Oded into his coat, pulled his green boots firmly onto his feet and said, 'Come on, Oded. You're going to bed. They won't bother you anymore.' And she added, 'No more running wild for them. Starting tonight, the night guard will do her job properly.'

They went out, leaving Roni alone in the apartment. He lit a cigarette and stood at the window, his back to the room, his face to the darkness outside. Leah returned at nine and didn't say a word to him. She sat down in her wicker armchair, smoked and read her education magazine. At ten Roni said, 'I'm going out for a walk. To see how he is.'

Leah said quietly, 'You're not going anywhere.'

Roni hesitated, then gave in because he no longer trusted himself.

At ten-thirty they turned off the radio, emptied the ashtray, opened the sofa and made up the double bed. They lay under their

98

separate blankets because tomorrow they had to get up for work before six again. Outside the rain had resumed and the wind blew the stubborn ficus tree branch against the shutters. Roni lay on his back for a while, his open eyes staring at the ceiling. For a moment he imagined that he heard a faint whistling in the darkness. He sat up in bed and listened hard, but now he could hear only rain and wind and the branch brushing against the shutters. Then he fell asleep.

At Night

In February it was Yoav Carni's turn to be night guard for a week, from Saturday to Friday. He had been Kibbutz Yekhat's first baby, and the founders, including his parents, were very proud when, years later, he was elected to be secretary — the first person to hold that post who was actually born on the kibbutz. Most of his friends were tanned, muscular and sturdy, while Yoav was gangly and slightly stooped, pale and big-eared, carelessly shaven, absent-minded and con-templative. He looked like a Talmudic scholar. His head always jutted forward as if he were examining the path before him, and his gaze was usually fixed beyond the shoulder of the person he was speaking to. He managed kibbutz matters with delicacy and tact. He never raised his voice or banged on the table, but the members knew that he was honest, quietly persistent and good-natured. He, for his part, was almost ashamed of his good nature and always tried to appear scrupulous, strict and zealously adherent to kibbutz principles. If you asked him for an easier job or fewer work hours, he would

103

answer gravely that such things were absolutely out of the question here and that we must always abide by our principles. But he would immediately begin a discreet search for a loophole, a way around the rules, in order to help you.

A few minutes before eleven at night, Yoav pulled on his boots and dressed warmly in his heavy, worn-out army jacket and a wool hat that covered his ears; then he went to the duty night guard, Zvi Provizor, to take over the rifle. Zvi, the gardener, said sadly to the secretary, 'Did you hear, Yoav? Minnesota is having its worst snowstorm in forty years. Eighteen dead and ten missing so far.'

Yoav said, 'I'm sorry to hear it.'

Zvi added, 'There are floods in Bangladesh too. And Rabbi Coopermintz died suddenly an hour or two ago in Jerusalem. They just announced it on the radio.'

Yoav reached out to pat Zvi on the shoulder but withdrew his hand when he recalled that Zvi didn't like to be touched. So he smiled at him instead, and said affectionately, 'If you should happen to hear one piece of good news, come and tell me right away. Even in the middle of the night.'

Yoav left, and when he passed the fountain that Zvi Provizor had installed in the square in front of the dining hall, he thought that a lonely, aging bachelor had a harder time here than he would in other places because kibbutz society offered no remedies for loneliness. In fact, the very idea of a kibbutz denied the concept of loneliness.

Now that he had taken the gun from Zvi, Yoav made his first round of the kibbutz grounds. As he walked past the old-timers' houses, he switched off lights that were burning needlessly here and there and turned off a sprinkler someone had forgotten before going to bed. He picked up an empty sack that had been tossed near the barber's shed, folded it carefully and left it at the door of the produce barn.

Lights still shone in some windows, but soon the kibbutz would be shrouded in sleep, and only he and the night guard in the children's house would stay awake till morning. A cold wind was blowing and the pine needles whispered in reply. A faint lowing came from the cow barn. In the darkness he made out the rows of buildings where the old-timers lived, four two-room apartments in each building, all furnished with plywood furniture, plants, floor mats and cotton curtains. At one o'clock he had to go to the brooder house to check the temperature, and at three-thirty he had to wake the dairy workers for the pre-dawn milking. The night would pass quickly.

Yoav enjoyed these night shifts, far removed from the daily routine full of committee discussions and members' complaints and requests. Sometimes people much older than he would come to pour out their hearts to him, and there were all sorts of delicate social problems requiring discreet solutions, or budget concerns, relationships with outside organisations, and kibbutz representation in the various institutions of the movement. Now, at night, he could wander alone among the lean-tos and chicken coops, stroll along the length of the fence illuminated by yellow lights, sit for a while on an upturned crate near the metalwork shop and sink into night thoughts. His night thoughts revolved around his wife Dana, now lying in the dark, listening drowsily to the radio in the hope that it would lull her to sleep; his mind also turned to their twins, now sleeping in their beds in the children's house. In an hour he'd stop in there and cover them. Maybe he'd also drop by his house and turn off the radio, which Dana usually neglected to do before she fell asleep. Dana didn't like living on the kibbutz and dreamed of a private life. She'd begged him to leave many times. But Yoav was a man of principle who fought constantly to improve kibbutz life and he wouldn't hear about leaving. Nonetheless, he knew in his heart that kibbutz life was fundamentally unjust to women, forcing them almost without exception into service jobs like cooking, cleaning, taking care of children, doing laundry, sewing and ironing. The women here were supposed to enjoy total equality, but they were treated equally only if they acted and looked like men: they were forbidden to use make-up and had to avoid all signs of femininity. Yoav had thought about that injustice many times, had tried to come to a conclusion about it, find a remedy, but could not. Perhaps that was why he always saw himself as the guilty party in his relationship with Dana and felt constantly apologetic.

The night was cold and clear. The croaking of frogs punctuated the silence and a dog barked somewhere far off. When Yoav looked up, he saw a mass of low clouds gathering above his head and said to himself that all the things we think are important really aren't, and he had no time to think about the things that really are. His whole life was going by and he had never contemplated the big, simple truths: loneliness and longing, desire and death. The silence was deep and wide, broken occasionally by the cries of jackals, and Yoav was filled with gratitude both for that silence and for the cries of the jackals.

He didn't believe in God, but in moments of solitude and silence such as this, Yoav felt that someone was waiting for him day and night, waiting silently and patiently, soundlessly and utterly still, and would wait for him always.

As he walked slowly between the cold-storage room and the fertiliser shed, the rifle slung over his shoulders, he saw a thin silhouette between the shadows of the walls and suddenly a figure wearing a coat blocked his path. A woman's voice, deep, pleasant, slightly husky, said, 'Don't be frightened, Yoav. It's just me. Nina. I've been waiting for you to pass by here. I knew you would. I have to ask you something.'

Yoav drew back, then focused his eyes in the darkness, pulled Nina by the arm to the nearby streetlamp and asked worriedly if she was cold and how long she'd been waiting there alone. Nina was a young woman known on the kibbutz for her strong, unwavering opinions. She had green eyes, long lashes and thin, finely sculpted lips. Her forehead shone in the dark and her blond hair was cropped short.

'Tell me what you would do, Yoav, if you had to live every day and sleep every night of your whole life with someone who repulses you. Has repulsed you for years. The things he says, his smell, his jokes, his scratching, his

108

hiccups, his coughing, his snoring, his nose-picking. Everything. What would you do?'

Yoav put his hand on her arm and said, 'Tell me exactly what happened, Nina.'

In the light of the streetlamp, he saw that her face was pale and tense, but her tired green eyes, looking straight into his, held not a single tear. She clenched her lips and said, 'Nothing happened. He even argues with the announcer on the radio.' Then she said, 'I can't take it any more.'

'Can we wait till tomorrow? Come to my office tomorrow and we'll talk? There are things that seem terrible at night but in the light of day they look completely different.'

'No. I won't go back to him. Not tonight, not ever. Give me a room tonight, Yoav. Even in a shed. In a lean-to. You must have one empty room.'

'Tell me what happened.'

'There's nothing to tell. I just can't go on any longer.'

'And the children?'

'The children will come straight to me from the children's house every afternoon. To the room you give me.'

Yoav felt uncomfortable standing and talking to Nina in the dim light of the streetlamp in the narrow alleyway between the cold-storage room and the fertiliser shed. If anyone happened to walk past and see them standing there, whispering, rumours would fly tomorrow. He said firmly, 'Nina. I'm sorry, but I really can't arrange something like this in the middle of the night. I don't have rooms in my pocket, you know. I'm not the one who allocates rooms here. The committee will have to discuss it. And I'm on guard duty now. Please go home to sleep and we'll meet tomorrow and try to find a solution together.'

But even as he spoke, he backtracked and found himself adding in a different tone of voice, 'Okay, come with me. We'll go to the office. There's a key to the lecturers' guest room hanging there. You can spend the night in the guest room and come back tomorrow so we can figure out what we can do. I'll speak to Avner tomorrow too.'

She leaned towards him, took his hand in both of hers and pressed it tightly against her breast. Yoav was embarrassed and even blushed slightly in the dark because Nina was an attractive woman who more than once had played a role in his secret fantasies. At seventeen he'd been in love with her for a while, but never dared approach her. At school Yoav had been a shy, introverted boy and Nina was already attracting the pick of the boys. Even now, her face etched with bitterness and fatigue and her body not as perfect as it used to be, she was still an attractive woman. We were all surprised when she married Avner Sirota, of all people, and bore him two sons. Avner was rowdy and given to brawling. His neck was so short that his square, shaven head seemed to rest heavily on his shoulders, and his arms were as beefy as a boxer's. He was a bit afraid of Nina, as if she knew an embarrassing secret about him. Even so, sometimes, in his coarse, joking way, he pursued high school girls behind her back. He was roughly affectionate with his two little boys and on summer nights encouraged them to wrestle with him on the lawn. He was always arguing politics in his hoarse voice, disparaging the heads of government, whom he dismissed as old-world weaklings. If they'd only given him and his paratrooper buddies a free hand for a month, he'd say, only a month to give the Arabs what they deserve, we'd have had peace and quiet here for a long time now. He'd stand in the square in front of the dining hall or on one of the paths, smoking and arguing with you, and Nina would wait beside him, head down, listening silently until she was sick and tired of it and put her hand on his back, interrupting him in her low, decisive voice, 'Avner. I think that's enough for today. Let's get going.'

Avner would immediately cut short his lecture and follow her. Roni Shindlin called them the little gypsy and her dancing bear.

Yoav asked, 'Won't Avner be looking for you?'

'He was asleep when I got dressed and left.'

'And if he wakes up and finds you gone?'

'He won't wake up. He never wakes up.'

'And when he gets up in the morning? Did you leave him a note?

'I have nothing to say to him. When he gets up in the morning he'll think I went to work early without waking him. We don't talk very much.'

'And later? What'll happen?

'I don't know.'

'There'll be a lot of talk. People will talk. The whole kibbutz will talk.'

'So let them.'

Yoav suddenly longed to press her slender body against his, or to unbutton his coat and draw her inside, or at least to caress her cheek. The urge was so strong that his hand reached out involuntarily and stroked the quivering air around her hair. He was cold, and he assumed that Nina was even colder because her head was bare and she was wearing thin shoes.

'Let's go,' he said. 'We'll find you a place for the night.'

She walked at his side, small, short-haired, half a step behind him because his stride was so long. He was a great deal taller than she and his shadow fell over hers. They passed the laundry and the shoemaker's shed. The smell of damp earth and chicken droppings floated on the cold air. Low dark clouds crawled over the roofs and there wasn't a star in the sky now. Yoav did a mental check of all the problems he'd have to deal with tomorrow and in the days that followed: Cheska had asked the kibbutz for permission to visit her family in Europe; Zvi Provizor needed a new lawnmower; Grandma Slava had bitten one of the kitchen workers; Roni Shindlin had gone into a children's house one night and beaten a five-year-old child; David Dagan had split up with Edna Asherov; they urgently needed to buy new equipment for the dental clinic; and now he also had to speak to Avner and find out if things could still be patched up, if this was a one-night crisis or another broken family.

Nina was three or four years younger than him, and when she was still a child she had impressed Yoav with her independent spirit and soft-spoken tenacity. She'd come to us an orphan, sent by her grandfather to go to school here. From her first day she was adamant in her opinions, and other people learned to respect her quiet persistence. At kibbutz meetings she was often the only one, or almost the only one, to oppose the general view. After her military service, she volunteered to work with groups of youth offenders in outlying towns. Since her return, she had been working alone in the apiary and had turned it into such a successful kibbutz enterprise that beekeepers from other kibbutzim came to learn from her. When it was her turn to go to college, she insisted on studying social work even though the kibbutz general meeting had voted to send her to a college for pre-school teachers. Nina headed the group of women on our kibbutz who rebelled against communal sleeping for young children, demanding that they spend their nights in their parents' apartment. The kibbutz general meeting did not accede to their demand and Nina was determined to raise the subject for discussion year after year until the majority saw it her way.

Two or three months after a paratrooper unit of the fighting pioneer youth joined the kibbutz, she chose from among their ranks Avner Sirota, hero of the retaliatory raid on Khirbet Jawad, and two months later she was pregnant. The kibbutz was surprised, even disappointed by her choice. Nevertheless, she was highly regarded among us because she knew how to listen silently and sympathetically and was always ready, in her quiet way,

114

to help anyone who needed it. When Boaz suddenly left Osnat and moved in with Ariella Barash, Nina went to live with Osnat for a few days. And when none of the girls would agree, under any circumstances, to work with Grandma Slava peeling vegetables on the back porch of the kibbutz kitchen, Nina volunteered to take on the job. Yoav still hadn't spoken to anyone about it, but he was thinking of suggesting at the general meeting that they elect Nina secretary when he completed his term. And perhaps tonight was only a temporary crisis and tomorrow morning she would see things differently. After all, she was a responsible, rational person. You don't break up a family just because your husband snores at night or insists on arguing with the radio announcer.

They crossed the dining-hall square, which was illuminated by several streetlights, walked round the fountain, and as they were passing the sleeping kindergarten, Tsippora, the night guard at the children's house, suddenly stopped them. She was about fifty-five, a wizened, angular woman who believed that the younger generation were destroying the kibbutz. Tsippora was surprised to see Dana Carni's husband and Avner Sirota's wife crossing the lawn together in the middle of the night. Concealing her surprise, Tsippora said, 'I don't want to bother you,' but asked nonetheless if they'd like to come into the children's kitchen for a late-night snack. Nina said, 'No, thank you,' and Yoav, embarrassed, apologised and began to mumble an explanation about some pressing matter that Nina simply had to clarify with him immediately. He knew that the words wouldn't help. By morning their names would fall straight out of Tsippora's mouth into the mouths of Roni Shindlin and his gossipy friends at their table in the far corner of the dining hall: so guess who our night guard is guarding at night?

'We're in a hurry to get something we need urgently from the office,' Yoav explained to Tsippora, and when they were out of earshot, said to Nina, 'They'll be talking about us tomorrow, the whole kibbutz will be talking.'

'I don't care, but I'm sorry for you.'

'And Avner?'

'Let him be jealous. I don't care.'

'I'll walk you back to the lecturers' guest room. Sleep a few hours and tomorrow we'll sit down and think about it again with a clear head.'

'My head has never been clearer than it is now.'

When they reached the office and Yoav turned on the light, he saw that the key to the lecturers' guest room wasn't hanging on the board. He remembered now that in the afternoon he'd given it to an Air Force officer who'd come to talk to the new recruits and was staying the night on Yekhat.

Yoav looked at Nina and Nina's sharp green eyes looked back at him, as if to say: surprise me. They stood close to each other in the office, which contained two desks with ordinary chairs, an upholstered bench, a metal cabinet full of files, a bare window, and on the wall a detailed aerial photo of the kibbutz and the agricultural land surrounding it. Before looking away from Nina's glance, Yoav noticed a fine wrinkle above her upper lip and thought it was a new one. And there were crow's feet around her tired eyes. He took in the delicate line of her chin and her severely short-cropped blond hair. He thought she looked strong, firm and resolute, definitely not in need of support. He was suddenly sorry that she wasn't broken and crushed. He could barely restrain the urge to reach out and pull her body to his, to feel the weight of her head against his chest. He fought against the wave of affection and longing that flooded him because he knew it wasn't fatherly affection, and in fact wasn't affection at all.

'You can spend the night here, on this bench,' he said. 'It's not very comfortable but I don't have any other place for you at the moment. Would you like me to make you a cup of tea? We have a kettle and cups here and even a few biscuits. I'll go and find you a blanket and a pillow.'

'Thank you. There's no need for a blanket and a pillow. I'm not going to sleep. I'm not tired. Just let me sit here till morning.'

Yoav turned on the electric heater and the kettle, left, and came back ten minutes later carrying a pillow and two woollen blankets. He found Nina pouring herself a cup of tea without asking if he wanted one too. He stood at the office door for a while, hesitating, his thin face reddening because he wanted to stay but knew he had to go, knew that before he went he should tell her something else, but didn't know what. Nina touched his shoulder with the tips of her fingers and said, 'Thank you.' Then she said, 'Don't worry. A little before six in the morning, before anyone comes, I'll leave to go to work in the apiary as usual. I'll make sure everything is in order here.'

And as if reading his mind, she added, 'No one will know that I spent the night here.'

Yoav hesitated, shrugged and said, 'Okay. So that's it for the time being.' And added, 'Goodnight.' Then, 'Still, you should try to sleep a little.'

He closed the door gently, and outside, pulled up his coat collar, strode across the soldiers' living area onto the muddy dirt path that led to the chicken coop to set the brooder house temperature, it being already one in the morning. On the side of the path he noticed a wet bush here and there, and a broken crate. He was sorry he didn't have a torch. The cold was more biting and the wind had intensified. Yoav thought about the darkness of the orchards on winter nights and he had a strong momentary urge to get up and leave everything, abandon his guard duty, walk to the orchards and wander alone in the dark among the now-bare fruit trees. Someone was waiting for him somewhere, or so he felt, someone had been waiting patiently for years, knowing that no matter how long Yoav delayed, he would ultimately come. One night he would get up and finally go. But where? That he didn't know, and was, in fact, a bit frightened of finding out.

On his way back from the chicken coop, he walked the length of the perimeter fence and checked the gate to the kibbutz, his collar pulled up, wool hat pulled down over his ears and rifle hanging on a strap from his shoulder. When he reached the children's house, he went inside to cover his twins and brush their foreheads with a kiss, then went from bed to bed, covering the other children too. Outside, he headed for his house, took his shoes off at the door and tiptoed inside to turn off the small bedside radio his wife kept on to lull her to sleep. Dana was asleep on her back, her dark curls spread softly on the pillow. Very gently, he straightened the blanket and, as if to apologise, he stroked a curl with the tips of his fingers and tiptoed out.

He wandered along the fence for about half an hour and when he noticed that the bulbs in two streetlamps had burned out, he made a mental note to tell Nahum Asherov, the electrician, about it tomorrow. At almost two o'clock a gibbous moon peeked out of the clouds, but still it began to drizzle. Yoav went to the children's kitchen for a cup of coffee with Tsippora, the night guard. He placed his rifle carefully on the floor but didn't take off his coat or hat, and sat down all bundled up. Tsippora poured black coffee, spread two slices of bread with margarine and jam, and said gloomily, 'It won't end well, Yoav, this thing of yours with Nina Sirota. Listen to what I'm telling you.'

'I have no thing with Nina Sirota. She just had an urgent problem and I had to help her solve it. Here, the secretary is still the secretary in the middle of the night.'

'It won't end well,' Tsippora insisted. 'A married man suddenly walking around with another man's wife in the middle of the night.'

'Tsippora. Listen to me for a minute. If you'd just keep it to yourself, please, and not talk about me and Nina tomorrow, you could help solve a delicate family problem. You're a responsible person and you must surely understand that you have to be discreet because this is a personal family problem.'

'Whose family problem? Yours or hers? Or both of yours?'

'Tsippora, please, I'm asking you. Let it go.'

But when he left the children's kitchen, he knew that his words would not help and tomorrow he and Nina would become the kibbutz subject of the day. He'd have to explain the night's events to Dana, who'd known for a long time that Yoav had once been a little in love with Nina. It would be complicated and messy.

The sky was purple-black and the clouds being pushed along by the wind looked heavy and dark. The entire kibbutz was deeply asleep. The fence lights painted pale yellow puddles. One of the lights, apparently about to die out, blinked as if in hesitation. Yoav stepped quietly through the shadows of the bushes and circled the hay barn, mud caking his shoes. You're so blind, he whispered to himself hopelessly, you're blind and deaf. He remembered the way Nina had leaned towards him when he promised to find her a room for the night and took his hand in hers and pressed it against her breast. You should have understood her intention and taken her in your arms. She was giving you a signal and you ignored it. And she gave you another hint in the office when she touched your shoulder with her fingertips, and you ignored it again.

His legs carried him across the square in front of the recreation hall and past the children's house on the way back to the kibbutz office next to the bus stop. He crossed the lawn in front of the dining hall. As if in a dream, he stopped and stood in front of the office window. Had she fallen asleep without turning off the light? Or was she still awake? On tiptoe, he approached the window and peered inside. Nina was lying on the bench covered with the woollen blankets he'd brought her, her blond head resting on the pillow, open eyes fixed on the ceiling. If he were to tap lightly on the window, she would startle and he didn't want to alarm her. So he backed away quietly and stood there, the rifle slung over his shoulder, among the cypress trees in the darkness. And asked himself but got no reply.

He could just knock on the door, go inside

and say, I saw that the light was still on and only came in to see if you need anything. Or: I came in to check that you're not cold. Or: I came in to see if you feel like talking for a while. All this time, she's been lying there on the other side of the wall with her eyes open, he thought, and maybe you're what she's waiting for and it's two in the morning now and the entire kibbutz is asleep.

He went back to the lit window, his hat down over his ears, head jutting forward, glasses glittering faintly in the dark as the light reflected off them, his heart going out to her but his legs planted firmly in place. Hadn't he been waiting all these years for just this moment? So why, instead of bursting with daring or passion, was he filling up with a vague sense of sadness? Then he walked silently round the building and stood for a while at the door, listening as hard as he could, hearing only the wind gusting through the pine needles. Finally, he sat down on the step in front of the door, pulled his hat even further down over his ears and waited. He sat like that for about half an hour, feeling that something was almost becoming clear to him, but what that something was he didn't know. A jackal cried from the darkness beyond; others answered it with a despairing sound from the direction of the orchard. He raised the rifle, his finger found the trigger, and only with the last vestige of his rational mind did he resist the urge to fire a long barrage into the air and tear the silence apart.

At three-thirty he stood up and went to wake the dairy workers for the pre-dawn milking. Then he did a last check along the fence and crossed the square back to the dining hall to turn on the electric samovar for the early-morning shift. The sun wouldn't rise until after six, and his guard duty ended at five. He still had to walk among the houses and wake the people whose names appeared on the list he had in his hand. There was no point in waiting for sunrise because it would most likely take place behind the mass of thick clouds. He had to go home now, shower, lie down, close his eyes and try to sleep. Tomorrow something might finally become clear to him.

Deir Ajloun

It was a sweltering, oppressive day. A low, dirty-grey sky hunched over us as if the desert had risen up and spread out upside down above the roofs of our small houses. The air was filled with fine dust that mixed with sweat and covered foreheads and arms with a sticky layer of whitish mortar. Henia Kalisch, a widow of about fifty, went into the bathroom during the lunch break, took off her work clothes and stood for a while under a torrent of cold water. Her lips were always tightly clenched and two bitter lines stretched from the corner of her lips to her chin. Her body was as angular and flat as a boy's and her legs were crisscrossed with blue and pink veins. The cold water washed off the dust and refreshed her skin, but did not allay the sense of malaise. After her shower she towelled herself brusquely, dressed again in her grey work shirt and navy-blue work trousers, then walked resolutely back to her shift in the kibbutz kitchen. That very evening she planned to talk to Yoav Carni the secretary, David Dagan the teacher, Roni and Leah Shindlin and a few other influential members of the kibbutz in an effort to drum up support for the vote at the general meeting on Saturday night.

On the back porch of the kitchen, bathed in sweat, they sat on stools across from each other peeling vegetables and slicing them into a large pot, and Brunia said to her, 'There's no point in bringing that up at the meeting, Henia. They'll bite your head off.'

Henia said, 'But it's good for everyone. The kibbutz'll be able to shorten the waiting list for college.'

Brunia chuckled, 'Your Yotam has no special standing here. No one does. Except for the select few.'

As she pushed away the pile of peelings and put a new crate of vegetables between them, Henia tried to sound out Brunia: 'But at least you, Brunia, you'll vote for Yotam's request at the Saturday night meeting, won't you? You'll support us, right?'

'Really? And why should I vote for him? When my Zelig asked to work in the vineyard six years ago, did you support him? You all voted against him. All you hypocrites and paragons together. Then you spoke so nicely at his funeral.'

Henia said, 'The pot is already full. We need to start a new one.' Then she added, 'Don't worry, Brunia. I have a very long memory, too. A very, very long memory.'

The two widows continued peeling and cutting vegetables in total silence, their knives glittering.

★   ★   ★

After work, Henia Kalisch returned to her apartment, showered with cold water again, shampooed her greying hair, and this time dressed in her afterwork clothes — a beige blouse, straight cotton skirt and lightweight sandals. She had coffee, cut two pears into slices exactly the same size and ate them slowly, washed her cup and plate, wiped them and put them in the cupboard. The windows and shutters were closed against the blazing heat and the curtains were pulled tightly shut. The room was dark and cool, and a pleasant clean smell rose from the washed floor tiles. She didn't turn on the radio because the arrogant voices of the news announcers made her angry: they always sound as if they know everything, and the truth is that no one really knows anything. People don't love each other anymore. At first, when the kibbutz was founded, we were all a family. True, even then there were rifts, but we were close. Every evening we'd get together and sing rousing songs and nostalgic ballads till the small

129

hours. Afterwards, we went to sleep in tents, and if anyone talked in their sleep, we all heard them. These days, everyone lives in a separate apartment and we're at each other's throats. On the kibbutz today, if you're standing on your feet, everyone is just waiting for you to fall, and if you fall . . . they all rush to help you up. Brunia is a monster and the whole kibbutz is right to call her a monster.

In her mind, Henia wrote a letter to her younger brother Arthur, who'd been living in Italy for a few years now and had become rich from his business there. She didn't know the nature of that business, but, putting two and two together, she thought it had something to do with spare parts for machines that manufactured weapons: in 1947, on the eve of the War of Independence, Arthur had been sent to Italy by the Haganah, with the consent of the kibbutz, to purchase arms for the underground and machines to manufacture light weapons for the nascent country. After the war he stayed in Italy, and, ignoring the anger of the kibbutz members and the general meeting's condemnation, he settled down in a suburb of Milan, where he began to spin the web of his shadowy business. In 1951 he sent Henia a picture of himself with his new wife, who was fifteen years younger than he was, an

Italian girl who looked soft and a bit mysterious in the photo because her thick black hair covered her eyes and she was hiding one of her cheeks with her hand. Several times he'd sent Henia small gifts.

Two weeks ago, Arthur wrote to her saying that he was going to ask Yotam to come and study mechanical engineering at the Milan Polytechnic Institute. He could live with him and Lucia, they had a large home, and he, Arthur, would pay the boy's tuition and all his living expenses for his four years at the Institute. Tell them on the kibbutz, Arthur wrote, that I'm saving them a lot of money because otherwise they'll have to pay Yotam's tuition and living expenses when it's his turn to go to college. With the money I save them they can send someone else to college. And I'll invite you too, Henia, to come and visit us once or twice a year.

Once, when Yotam was about six, Uncle Arthur came for a visit, on a Haganah motorcycle, and took him for a ride around the kibbutz. How surprised and envious the other children were when they saw him sitting pressed up against his uncle's strong body, which gave off a pungent, pleasing smell of pipe tobacco when he held him high in the air and said, 'Grow up, grow older, be a soldier.'

Yotam was short, tanned and muscular,

broad and sturdy, and his roundish head was topped with hair clipped almost to the roots. He had large, very strong hands. He wasn't good-looking, and when he was spoken to a faint expression of wonder spread across his face, as if all the words directed at him surprised or frightened him. A missing front tooth, along with his wrestler's body, made him look belligerent. But contrary to his appearance, Yotam was a shy young man who spoke little, though from time to time he would suddenly come out with a strange, sweeping statement. On the kibbutz we called him a philosopher because he once emerged from his silence to claim that man has the basic nature of a freakish animal. Another time, at dinner in the kibbutz dining hall, he said that there were more similarities than differences between humans, animals, plants and inanimate objects. Roni Shindlin's response to that, given behind Yotam's back, was that Yotam Kalisch himself really did bear a slight resemblance to a box or a packing crate.

Yotam had been discharged from the army about six months before his Uncle Arthur's letter, and went to work in the orchards. He wasn't an outstanding worker; there was a certain languor about him. But his co-workers were impressed by his great physical strength

132

and his willingness to work overtime when necessary. When Uncle Arthur's letter arrived from Italy, Yotam delayed for two or three days, then finally said to his mother in a low voice, as if admitting guilt for some crime, 'Yes, but only if the kibbutz agrees.'

Henia said, 'It'll be hard to get a majority at the meeting. There'll be a lot of jealousy and resentment.'

Roni Shindlin said to his regular table-mates in the dining hall, 'What a shame that rich uncles in Italy are in such short supply these days. It wouldn't hurt if we each had one. Then we could send all the young people to college at his expense. Problem solved.'

And David Dagan, the teacher, said to Henia that he would oppose Yotam's request for three reasons. First, on principle, every young man and woman has to work on the kibbutz for at least three years after the army and only then can the possibility of college be considered. Otherwise there won't be anyone left here to milk the cows. Second, such gifts from rich relatives strike a serious blow against the principle of equality. Third, the young people who leave to attend college should study something that will benefit our society and our enterprises here on the kibbutz. What do we need a mechanical engineer for? We have two mechanics working in the garage and they're doing just fine without a certified professor there.

Henia tried in vain to soften David Dagan, citing young people's innate right to self-fulfillment. David Dagan chuckled and said, 'Self-fulfillment, self-fillfulment, it's nothing but self-indulgence. Just give me a minute so we can set things straight: either every one of us, without exception, gives an eight-hour work day six days a week or there'll be no kibbutz here at all.'

That evening, Henia went to see Yoav Carni, the secretary, in his apartment and told him that she had to put all her cards on the table: if the kibbutz meeting on Saturday night didn't let Yotam accept his Uncle Arthur's invitation to go to college in Italy, there was a chance he might go anyway, without their permission. 'Do you really want to lose him? Don't any of you care at all?' This ultimatum was entirely Henia's idea because Yotam had, of course, told her the opposite, that he would accept Uncle Arthur's invitation only if the kibbutz agreed.

Yoav Carni asked, 'Why did you come here, Henia? Why doesn't Yotam himself come to talk to me?'

'You know Yotam. He's a boy who keeps things close. Introverted. He has inhibitions.'

'If he's brave enough to go to college in

134

Italy without knowing the language and without friends, he should have enough courage to come here himself and not send his mother.'

'I'll tell him to come and see you.'

'Okay, good. But I'm afraid he won't hear from me what he wants to hear. I'm against private initiatives and private funds in the life of the kibbutz. Yotam has to wait his turn, and when it comes, the Higher Education Committee, along with him, will decide where and how he goes to college and what he studies. When the time comes, if his uncle wants to help pay expenses, we'll discuss it and take a vote. That's our way. Those are the rules. But tell him to come and see me and I promise to listen to him and then explain these things patiently. Yotam is a sensitive, intelligent young man and I'm sure he'll understand our position and withdraw his request of his own free will.'

The faint, oppressive smell of plants sweating in the blistering heat lay over the kibbutz lands. The hot, dusty air was stagnant. The ficus and pine trees, the myrtle bushes, the bougainvillea and ligustrum shrubs, the lawns and rose beds all breathed heavily in the darkness under the dense, blazing mass. A gust of arid air mixed with the smell of scorched thorns blew down from the hilltop ruins of the abandoned Arab village of Deir Ajloun. Perhaps distant fires were still burning there. At nine at night, without knocking, Henia walked into Yotam's room, which was in one of the sheds in the discharged soldiers' housing area, and told him that the meeting on Saturday night was probably going to reject his request. They'd most likely decide to tell Uncle Arthur that if he wanted to support the education of Kibbutz Yekhat's youth, he was invited to contribute to the kibbutz college fund.

'They're fanatics, all of them,' Henia said. 'They're jealous. Resentful.'

Yotam said, 'Okay.' Then added, 'Thank you.' After a brief silence, he said, 'You shouldn't have spoken to them, Mother. It's too bad you did. Mechanical engineering isn't really for me, anyway.'

The night was still gravid and dusty. The thick, inert desert air pressed down on everything. Mosquitoes buzzed around them and two or three moths slammed into the naked light bulb dangling from the ceiling. The tin roof radiated the heat of the day into the room and no coolness came in at the open window. Yotam's room was furnished with an iron bedstead, a wooden table painted green, a curtain-covered crate used as a closet, a straw floor-mat and two or three wicker stools. An electric fan stood in a corner of the room, stirring the air to no avail. Visible through the window were the hills which concealed the ruins of Deir Ajloun. Both mother and son were bathed in sweat. The stubble on Yotam's head, his muscular shoulders, his tanned, broad back in a blue singlet and his missing front tooth lent him an air of coiled violence he didn't possess. His almost unnaturally large hands rested heavily on his naked knees. He sat on the unmade bed and his mother on one of the stools. Yotam offered her cold water from the jug that stood under the window, but Henia refused with a dismissive wave of her hand, as if she were swatting a fly.

'Go and talk to Yoav. I don't think anything will come of it; I've already spoken to him, but you should try anyway.'

'I won't talk to Yoav, Mother. There's no point. They'll never let me go.' After a brief silence he added, 'I'd like to travel to Italy. Or maybe not to Italy in particular. Just somewhere. But mechanical engineering is not for me.'

'But you want to go to college, don't you? And Arthur is offering to pay for it.'

'What I want, more or less, is not to live here for a few months. Maybe a year. Maybe two. Then we'll see.'

'You want to leave the kibbutz?'

'I don't know. I didn't say leave. I said travel. We'll see. I only know that I need to go away, at least for a while.'

'Do you even remember Arthur?'

'No. Almost not at all. I remember that he liked to tell jokes all the time. I remember pipe smoke. And that he once brought me skates as a gift and the Education Committee decided that they would belong to all the kids in my class. And I know, too, that the whole kibbutz is still angry with him since the time he refused to come back here and decided to stay in Italy.'

Henia said, 'Your brother Gideon finished the army, worked quietly for three years in the fodder fields, got married, had a child and waited his turn, and then the kibbutz sent him to study agriculture at the Ruppin Institute. But you won't wait. You can leave now and you will leave now. What do you care what the general meeting decides? You'll come back here an engineer and they can all eat their hearts out. Or maybe you won't come back.'

'I can't take it here anymore, Mother. Arthur invited me and I want to go. But only if the general meeting agrees. And no mechanical engineering.'

Henia said, 'They won't agree. The air is full of spite.'

The sour smell of rotten, fermenting

orange peel and the stench of cow dung coming from the direction of the barn filled the room. A malicious mosquito buzzed piercingly next to Henia's ear. She slapped herself hard in a vain attempt to squash it. Finally she said, 'You don't know what you want yourself. Go to the office tomorrow and talk to Yoav Carni. Yoav is a sympathetic person. Maybe together you'll find some kind of compromise.'

Yotam didn't want to talk to the secretary. In fact, he didn't want to talk to anyone. Not his mother either. What he wanted was to go out for a walk. Several times, in the early evening, he'd wandered alone among the ruins of Deir Ajloun for almost an hour. He went into the destroyed mosque and the dynamited sheikh's house but found nothing there because he didn't know what he was looking for, so, shoulders hunched, he walked back to the kibbutz. He had a vague desire now to return and examine the ruins, as if something were buried there under the avalanche of rocks or in the darkness of the blocked well, a simple answer. But what the question was he didn't know.

Some people on our kibbutz thought that Yotam Kalisch was hopelessly in love with Nina Sirota, who was five or six years older than he was and had separated from her husband several months earlier. When she left her apartment and moved in to a room the Apartment Committee allocated to her at the far end of the Housing Area 3, Yotam went there one day after work in the orchards and, without saying a word, turned the soil in her new garden with a pitchfork. More than once we saw him linger at the door to the dining hall till she came out, then follow her along the kibbutz paths until his courage failed him and he turned onto a side path and walked away. He almost never dared to talk to her, but sometimes went to the carpentry shop in the evening and made small wooden toys for her children. In his huge hands the toys looked like miniatures. When a notice was hung on the bulletin board at the dining hall entrance calling for members to sign up for special work on Saturdays, we noticed that Yotam waited for Nina to sign up, then put his name down for work on the same Saturday she had chosen. But when they were actually working together, he almost never spoke to her. Only once did he summon the courage to ask her among the rows of vines, 'Is the heat bothering you, Nina?' And she replied with a smile, 'No, everything's fine, thank you.'

She was always pleased to see him, and when they met on the path, she asked how he was, how his mother was and what was new in the orchards. Actually, it wasn't just Yotam she was pleased to see. She was cordial to everyone on the kibbutz, even the children. There was always an air of pleasant warmth about her when, with a smile, she'd say the most ordinary words to you, such as good evening, how are you, what's new?

Roni Shindlin said, 'Here we go again. Another broken heart. The caterpillar has fallen in love with the butterfly.'

Nina was appreciated for her confident opinions and her willingness to go up against the prevailing view. She had introduced a subversive element of constant restlessness at the general meetings, and it seemed that the secretary, Yoav Carni, supported her on one issue or another, to the great chagrin of the conservatives. Working on her own in the apiary, she had continued to make it a profitable branch of Kibbutz Yekhat. At the kibbutz meetings, she often fought for her view that the men had to take on a larger part of the service work in the kitchen, laundry and children's houses so that the women would be free to go out and work in the fields. When she left her husband, Avner Sirota, some people said, 'That girl only knows how to break things.' Others said, 'That girl has decided to be head of the opposition on Kibbutz Yekhat.'

And still others said, 'Who does she think she is?'

Since Nina Sirota had sought out Yoav Carni, the kibbutz secretary, the night he was on guard duty, their relationship had become one of cautious fondness and heightened awareness. Sometimes he asked her advice about matters on the kibbutz agenda. He didn't always agree with her opinion, but he always found her to be original, lucid and trustworthy. Early one Thursday evening he found her sitting on a bench in the garden watching her children play in the sandpit. He sat down on her left and they spoke a bit about the heat and the problem with the swimming pool. Then, as if reading his mind, Nina said that at the meeting on Saturday night it might be a good idea to try and find a compromise on the question of Yotam's trip to Italy. After all, when the time came, the kibbutz would send him to college anyway. And now that his uncle had invited him, maybe they should let him go before it was his turn, but only if he learned a profession the kibbutz chose together with him, instead of the irrelevant one his uncle had chosen. Yoav asked, 'For example?'

Nina replied, 'For example, veterinary medicine. We have cows, sheep and chickens here, not to mention our pets, and a vet comes from the city at least once a week. Yotam can study veterinary medicine in Italy. When he gets his degree, he can come back to Yekhat and be our vet and work in other villages in the area too. Why not?' Then she added, 'I think he'd make a very good vet.'

Yoav thought about it for a moment, shrugged and said that they might be able to sell the idea, though it wouldn't be easy, and only if Yotam agreed to postpone his trip for two years until it was his turn to go to college.

Nina said, 'One year?'

Yoav shook his head, opened his mouth, closed it, hesitated and finally said, 'We could try. I'll talk to him. The problem is that his mother is pressuring the whole kibbutz, making everyone angry and turning public opinion against him. And the second problem is that all the old-timers are still furious with Arthur because they think he deserted the kibbutz when he was sent to Italy. Yotam is a little in love with you, isn't he? Maybe you should talk to him?'

'I like him too, but I'm not sure I want to talk to him about this. I think I'll embarrass him too much. It's better if you speak to him. Have you noticed that he has no friends?'

Yoav said, 'On the kibbutz it's hard to know. We're all supposed to be friends, but

143

only very few really are. Take me, for example. I only have two or three personal friends, people I enjoy being with even if we don't talk. I don't think you have more than that either.' He had a strong urge to tell her that what they, he and Nina, had together was close to what he considered friendship, but he hesitated, then decided not to say it.

'In ten or twenty years,' Nina said, 'the kibbutz will be a much more relaxed place. Now all the springs are tightly coiled and the entire machine is still shaking from the strain. The old-timers are actually religious people who left their old religion for a new one that's just as full of sins and transgressions, prohibitions and strict rules. They haven't stopped being true believers, they've simply exchanged one belief system for another. Marx is their Talmud. The general meeting is the synagogue and David Dagan is their rabbi. I can easily picture some of the men here with beards and sidelocks, and some of the women in head coverings. But slowly, times will change and other, more relaxed people will come, and like you, Yoav, they'll be people with patience and doubts and compassion.'

'You're completely wrong about me, Nina. I also have principles that I try not to deviate from. I also think that the kibbutz can't exist without a framework and rules and basic principles. Veterinary medicine, maybe, yes, it's an idea. And it suits Yotam much more than mechanical engineering. Yes. Maybe. But not now. In two years, when it's his turn to go to college. That I might be able to push through at the meeting on Saturday night. Not mechanical engineering and not now, but veterinary medicine in another two years.'

'One?'

'It'll be difficult. There'll be a huge battle at the meeting. David Dagan will sound off. The old-timers will object on principle to taking money from the uncle — they despise Arthur — and the young people will probably be split on the vote. It'll be difficult and complicated, Nina.'

On Saturday morning, the day the kibbutz general meeting was scheduled to discuss and vote on the matter of Yotam's attending college in Italy, David Dagan went to Yotam Kalisch's room. Yotam, who'd slept late, was still in bed clad only in underpants and a vest, and his huge hands pulled the sheet over the lower half of his body to hide his morning erection. David was wearing sharply creased khaki trousers and a light-blue, short-sleeved shirt with a battery of three pens sticking out of the breast pocket. He had very straight, almost military, posture and his shoulders were strong and square. His full head of greying hair was tousled just enough to look dashing but not completely unkempt. David, who'd been Yotam's teacher a few years ago, gave him an offhand hello and sat down on the edge of the rumpled bed. Yotam hesitated and, moving awkwardly under his sheet, pulled on the work trousers he picked up from the floor, then leaned over and turned on the electric fan. David scrutinised him until he was finished and had sat up, then gestured for him to take a seat on one of the wicker stools. Yotam obediently moved over to the stool.

'I'm worried,' David began without pre-amble, 'about Henia. She's taking all this very hard. You've put your mother in a difficult position with our members.'

Yotam was silent and stared at the window.

'And just when I've been hearing that you're doing such an outstanding job in the orchards.'

Yotam remained silent.

'Do you want to be a mechanical engineer?'

'Not exactly, but . . . '

'But you feel suffocated here and the big world is so alluring,' David said, without a question mark at the end of his sentence. 'You'll be surprised to hear that I also find the big world alluring. I'd love to see Rome, Florence, Venice, Naples.'

Yotam shrugged. David put a hand on his

knee and said quietly, 'But every Jew of the generation that witnessed the Holocaust, and especially now, so soon after the rebirth of the State of Israel, must see himself as mobilised to a cause. These are the most critical years in the entire history of the Jewish people.'

Yotam said, 'The thing is I can't take it anymore. I have no air.'

David looked at Yotam with affection and curiosity. Then he said, 'All right. Go.' And added, 'Just give me a minute to set things straight. At tonight's meeting, I'll recommend that the kibbutz grant you two or three weeks off out of consideration for your personal crisis. Go to Italy. See your uncle. Breathe some new air. Then return to us with renewed energy and go back to your job in the orchards.'

Yotam tried to say something, but David Dagan placed a fatherly hand on his shoulder and interrupted him, 'Please, think it over. Think it over till tonight.' And as he was leaving he said, 'Don't force the kibbutz to slam the door in your face tonight, Yotam, and especially not in Henia's face. Think calmly about my offer. Please decide by tonight.'

★ ★ ★

At two in the afternoon, when the oppressive heat had crushed the life out of everything and the low sky was a polluted grey colour, Yotam left his room and walked down the paved path through Housing Area 3, past the cow barns and the chicken coops. There was no one outside because they were all having their Saturday afternoon rest. Not a single living soul saw him except for a thirsty dog, and Yotam stopped for moment to turn on the garden tap for it. The dog lapped up the water noisily, its head and snout getting wet in the flow. Then it shook itself, spraying water in every direction, panted, wagged its tail rapidly and knelt down on its front legs as if prostrating itself in front of Yotam. He petted the animal distractedly, then continued walking across the heat-choked lawns and among trees that looked inanimate because no wind touched them.

Passing Nina Sirota's apartment, he quickened his steps, hoping she wouldn't happen to emerge just then, wishing at the same time that the door would open and she'd come out and talk to him about Italy and perhaps understand him. Even though he really had no idea what he could say to her. The entire kibbutz was talking about his request to be sent to Italy, and that night he'd stand in front of everyone and the secretary would give him the floor and three hundred pairs of eyes would glare at him, and he still had no idea what he could say. And if Nina came out of her apartment this very moment? What could he say to her?

Piles of slop lay between the cow barns, and old tyres and bits of scrap metal were scattered on the ground along with a few discarded, rusty milking pails. Yellowing bits of newspaper were trapped among the nettles and bindweed that grew between the barns. Yotam crossed the area of the barns and coops and went out to the fields through the back gate, known on the kibbutz as the Dung Gate. The path soon led to a ploughed field on the right and a vineyard on the left, both swathed in dust because of the intense, dry heat. Very quickly Yotam felt the dust slip beneath his clothes and stick to his sweaty skin. Not a single breath of wind stirred the congealed air. He lingered at the cemetery, thinking for a moment that he might visit the grave of his father, who had died of kidney disease when Yotam was eleven, but then he decided to sit on the bench at the cemetery gate for five minutes. He thought about his father, one of the kibbutz founders, who had spent his life working in the sheep pen. He'd been seriously injured in the War of Independence on the night Kibbutz Yekhat was invaded and burned to the ground by an Arab mob from Deir Ajloun and the nearby villages. Six weeks later, the tables were turned and Deir Ajloun was destroyed by the Israeli army, all the inhabitants driven off to the mountains and their fields divided among the kibbutzim in the area. Then Yotam thought about Arthur, who'd dared to disobey the general meeting, had cut off all contact with the kibbutz and the country and refused to serve the cause when the war was over. He'd built the life that he, and only he, had wanted. I can get up and go too and build the life I want. David Dagan said that in this generation, the generation of the Holocaust and Israel's War of Independence, each of us must be mobilised to the cause. Yotam could find no argument against that claim. But suddenly the phrase 'his days are as grass' came into his head and made him think how fleeting life is.

He stood up and walked for another twenty minutes along the path that wound between the ploughed fields until he was in the hills. For some reason Yotam thought that here, in the hills, the heat would be less brutal than on the plains. But the thorns, the prickly cacti that grew along the side of the road and the exposed rocks on the slopes seemed to smoulder, and Yotam felt as if he were drowning in sweat. His throat was dry and rough, and his feet in their open sandals were rubbed raw by the mixture of sweat and sand.

At three in the afternoon, when the predatory sun was crushing the ruins and boiling the soil and the stones, Yotam reached the destroyed village of Deir Ajloun. He wandered around for forty minutes or so, ran his hands over the vestiges of the decapitated mosque, bent over to pick up a piece of earthenware that had once been the neck of a jar, passed a grindstone half-buried in the ground. He wandered along paths strewn with pottery shards and thorns. A frightened lizard darted past his feet. And the smell of smoke hung in the air like an echo; it wasn't clear to Yotam where that smell was coming from, perhaps from thorns burning somewhere in the distance. Finally he reached the blocked well with the faint stench of dead animals rising from its depths. Yotam sat down on the edge of the well and waited, though he didn't know what he was waiting for or why. He heard the sounds of the kibbutz in the distance, strange, melancholy noises that seemed to come to him through a thick stone wall: a dull beating; the clang of metal against metal; the faint barking of dogs; the whirring of a raspy motor, maybe a

151

tractor someone was having trouble starting; and also a person's voice shouting and shouting beyond the distance and the blazing heat. He leaned over the well, saw only darkness and thought he heard a steady, unbroken murmur, the soft whisper of a distant sea, the sound you hear when you put a seashell to your ear. For a moment, he imagined that he had already left the kibbutz and gone off to a new life, a life without committees, general meetings, public opinion or the-fate-of-the-Jews. A moment later he thought of Nina Sirota and asked himself if she, like almost everyone else on the kibbutz, would have voted against him tonight. Then he answered his own question: neither Nina nor anyone else on the kibbutz had any reason to support his request, and if it had come from any of the other young people he himself might have thought, what makes him so special, and would have voted with the nays. It was clear to him now that the real issue wasn't Arthur's invitation but whether he had enough courage to leave the kibbutz, his mother and his brother, and go out into the world with only the shirt on his back. To that question he found no answer. Thorns and dry leaves stuck to his clothes and he stood up and brushed off his trousers and shirt. Then he began to walk, though what he wanted more than anything was to remain sitting there among the ruins of Deir Ajloun, on the edge of the blocked well, to sit there utterly still, his mind empty of thoughts, and to wait.

Esperanto

Martin Vandenberg's neighbour, Osnat, stopped by to see him one evening carrying a tray set with a plate covered with another plate and a cup covered with a saucer. Martin lived alone and had a respiratory condition, the result of years of smoking. In the afternoon, he would sit on his small porch and read the paper, occasionally breathing through a mask attached to an oxygen tank because his lungs were failing. He sometimes used the mask at night too. Nonetheless, when he had the strength, he got up at six in the morning and went to work for three or four hours in the shoe-repair shop. He was a firm believer in the principle that we must all devote ourselves to physical labour. 'Work,' he said, 'is a moral and spiritual necessity.'

'I've brought you something light from the dining hall. How about putting the paper down now and eating?'

'Thank you. I'm not hungry.'

'You have to eat. Just the omelette and the salad.'

'Maybe later.'

'Later the omelette'll be cold and the

salad'll lose its crispness.'

'I'm getting cold and losing my crispness too. Thank you, Osnat. Really. You don't have to worry about me.'

'So who will?'

For several months now, ever since Boaz left her and moved in with Ariella Barash, Osnat had been living alone next door. Early every evening she'd bring Martin supper on a tray because the uphill walk to the dining hall had become too difficult and left him short of breath. He had come to us, alone, from another kibbutz, where all the members were from Holland. He had left them over an ideological disagreement: they allowed Holocaust survivors to keep part of their German reparation money in private bank accounts, while Martin, also a survivor, thought that property was original sin, especially reparations from Germany, which amounted to blood money.

A stubborn, opinionated man, he was thin and had frizzy grey hair as stiff as steel wool, small eyes that were black and penetrating, thick eyebrows, sunken cheeks and stooped shoulders. His breathing was loud and raspy from the emphysema. But, despite the disease, he occasionally smoked half a cigarette, wheezed and refused to give in. He had taught Esperanto in Rotterdam when he was a young man, but since his arrival in Israel in 1949 he'd had no opportunity to use that remarkable language. The small Esperanto course he had wanted to give here on Kibbutz Yekhat had never panned out. It was his belief that states should be abolished and replaced by an international, pacifist brotherhood that would reign after the borders between peoples were erased. When he came to us, he wanted to learn how to be a shoemaker, and not only did a fine job of repairing our shoes, but also made children's shoes and sandals himself. Dr Shoemaker, we called him.

On the kibbutz he was considered a model of morality. At general meetings he often reminded us of why the kibbutz movement was founded and what its original ideals had been. Nevertheless, there were those who thought him odd because in all the years he'd been with us, he had never missed a single day of work. If he took sick and had to stay in bed for a day or two, he'd open the shoe repair shop on Saturdays to give the community back the time he'd missed. He believed that the entire world would wake up one day soon and abolish money altogether, since money was the root of all evil, a constant cause of war, conflict and exploitation. On top of all this, he was also a vegetarian. Roni Shindlin, the comedian, called him the Gandhi of Kibbutz Yekhat.

Two years ago, Roni came to our Purim costume party dressed up as Martin Vandenberg. He wore a white sheet and dragged a goat behind him with a sign in Esperanto hanging round its neck that said: *I'm a person too.*

Osnat said, 'If you eat, I'll stay with you for a while. And I'll play two or three songs for you until you fall asleep.'

'I'm not hungry.'

'If you eat at least half the omelette, I'll play you one song, and if you eat half the omelette and some yoghurt, I'll play you two, and if you eat the salad and the bread too, you can give me a short lecture.'

'You can go. Go. There's music outside, lots of young men, and there's dancing. Go.'

But a moment later, he relented, 'Okay. Okay. You win. I'll eat a little. Here, see for yourself. I'm eating.'

Osnat had brought a simple recorder with her, the kind we give to young children, and as he ate she played 'On the Shore of Lake Kinneret' and 'They Say There's a Land'. Martin ate a few mouthfuls of the omelette and a little yoghurt, grimaced, and didn't touch the salad or the bread, but let Osnat help him sip some of the lukewarm tea from the cup she'd brought from the dining hall. On principle, he didn't keep a private kettle or cups in his room: accumulating possessions is the curse of human society; it is the nature of possessions slowly to take over the soul and enslave it. Nor did Martin believe in the institution of family, because a family unit, by its very nature, creates an unnecessary barrier between itself and society. He believed that the community, not the biological parents, should raise the children: everything here belongs to all of us, we all belong to each other and the children should belong to all of us, too.

Martin Vandenberg's room was furnished with Spartan simplicity: a bed, a table, a large curtain-covered crate to hang his clothes in, and another elongated crate on iron legs that served as a bookcase. It was filled with books in six languages on philosophy and academic research, four or five novels in German, Dutch and Esperanto, several volumes of poetry, a number of dictionaries, and a bible with illustrations by Gustave Doré. Hanging on the wall was a picture of Ludwig Lazarus Zamenhof, the creator of Esperanto, the language that everyone on all five continents would speak someday so that the barriers between individuals and peoples would be brought down and the world could return to the way it was before the curse of the Tower of Babel.

Osnat helped Martin to his bed and stroked his forehead gently. She left a small lamp burning at his bedside and switched off the ceiling light. Martin didn't sleep lying down but sitting up, his head and shoulders supported by large pillows to ease his breathing. Every night he'd sit that way on his bed waiting for sleep which, if it came, was brief and fragmented. Osnat placed the oxygen mask over his nose and mouth, the grey stubble on Martin's sunken cheeks jutting out from under it. She smoothed his blanket and asked if he needed anything else. From behind his mask Martin said, 'No. Thank you. You're an angel.'

Then he took off the mask and said, 'Man is by nature good and generous. It's only the injustices of society that push him into the arms of selfishness and cruelty.' And added, 'We must all become as innocent as children again.'

From where she stood at the door, Osnat replied, 'Children are spoiled, cruel, selfish creatures. Just like we are.'

However, since neither of them had children, and because they didn't want to end their evening with an argument, neither one added anything further to their disagreement but simply said goodnight. After she'd gone, the small lamp next to Martin's bed continued to burn. He pulled a pack of cigarettes out from under his pillows and, taking advantage of Osnat's departure, smoked half a cigarette, crushed the butt in an ashtray, wheezed a little, then put the oxygen mask back over his face, his breathing rapid and shallow. Leaning against the pillows, he read a book by a well-known Italian anarchist who maintained that authority and obedience to that authority are contrary to man's nature. Then he dozed off in his semi-upright position, the transparent mask covering the bottom half of his face, the light still on. It remained burning next to his bed till morning, even though Martin believed that waste was exploitation and frugality a moral imperative. But the dark terrified him.

Osnat took the tray with her when she left, though most of the food was still on it. She put it down on the porch steps to take it back to the kibbutz kitchen early the next morning on her way to work in the laundry. Then she went for a short walk along the cypress-lined avenue, which was illuminated by the garden lights. Ever since Boaz had left her to go and live with Ariella Barash, Osnat had become especially attentive to everything around her, to the words of passersby and the sounds of birds and dogs. As she walked, she thought she heard Martin choking and calling for her to come back, but she realised that it was only her imagination, because even if he were calling her, she wouldn't have been able to hear him from that distance.

Sitting alone on a bench in the middle of the avenue of cypress trees was Grandma Slava, wearing a loose cotton dress and open sandals that showed her coarse, crooked, red toes. A widow and bereaved mother, she was feared by one and all on the kibbutz — they called her a witch and a monster because she was always telling people off and had been known to spit in the face of anyone who made her angry. Osnat said good evening and Grandma Slava asked her in a mocking, bitter tone, 'So what exactly is it that makes this hot and humid evening so good?'

Back in her apartment, Osnat poured herself a glass of cold water with lemon syrup and took off her sandals. She stood barefoot at the open window and said to herself that most people seem to need more warmth and affection than others are capable of giving, and none of the kibbutz committees will ever be able to cover that deficit between supply and demand. The kibbutz, she thought, makes small changes in the social order but man's difficult nature doesn't change. A committee vote will never be able to eradicate envy, pettiness or greed.

She washed her glass and placed it upside down on the drying rack, undressed and went to bed. Only a thin wall separated her bed from Martin's, and she knew that if he coughed or wheezed at night she'd wake up immediately, throw on her robe and hurry next door to help him. She was a very light sleeper; her ears registered every bark of a dog in the darkness, every shriek of a night bird, every sigh of wind in the thick bushes. But the night passed quietly, with only the sound of the night winds blowing through the ficus trees. Towards dawn, heavy dew fell on the lawns and the moonlight poured over everything, illuminating the glistening, pale-silver dewdrops.

The pigeons woke Osnat before six, as usual, and she showered, dressed, knocked on Martin's door to see how he was, picked up yesterday's tray and went to work in the laundry. Martin got out of bed and dressed slowly, panting from the effort as he bent to put on his shoes. After drinking some water, he set out for the shoe-repair shop, pushing his small oxygen tank in the old pram the Health Committee had allocated to him. He walked slowly, dragging his feet, because he found it hard to breathe, especially going uphill. Near the electrician's workshop he met Nahum Asherov, the electrician, and the two men spoke for a while about politics and Ben Gurion's government. Nahum said that the government was provoking the whole world with its retaliatory raids, and Martin replied that all governments, without exception, are completely unnecessary and our government was doubly unnecessary because the Jews had already shown the world how a people can exist and even thrive spiritually and socially for thousands of years without any government at all. As he spoke, Martin lit half a cigarette, but didn't inhale more than twice because he began to choke. He put it out and returned the butt to his pocket.

Nahum Asherov said, 'Don't smoke, Martin. You shouldn't smoke.'

'We shouldn't tell others what they should or shouldn't do,' Martin replied. 'We were all born free, but we shackle each other with our very own hands.'

'We have to look out for each other,' Nahum said, with a sigh.

A smile crossed Martin's sunken lips. 'So be it, Nahum. You definitely have to tell me not to smoke and I definitely have to smoke. Each of us does what he's meant to do. So be it.'

In the shoe-repair shed, sitting on a wicker stool and surrounded by the pungent odours of leather, polish and glue, Martin placed the oxygen tank on a crate beside him and pulled the mask over his face. Then, holding a cobbler's sharp knife in his fist, he cut out a precise left sole along the line he had drawn in pencil earlier on a sheet of leather. A small bottle of lukewarm water stood on the floor in front of him, and every now and then he lowered the mask slightly and took two or three sips. Work, he said to himself, returns us to the simplicity and purity of our early childhood. An old Spanish melody, the anthem of the Republican soldiers from the days of the Spanish Civil War, came to his mind and Martin hummed it softly.

A little after eight in the morning, Yoav Carni, the kibbutz secretary, came in and said, 'I'm here to bother you for a few minutes. We need to talk.'

Martin said, 'Sit down, young man.' Then he moved the oxygen tank from the crate to the floor at his feet and added, 'There aren't too many places to sit here. Sit on the crate.'

Yoav sat down and Martin apologised for not having any coffee to offer him. Yoav thanked him and said that there was no need for coffee. Martin thought Yoav was an honest, dedicated and modest young man, but, like the others of his generation, he had no clearly defined world view. They were all good men, Martin believed, all decent and ready to take on hard work of any kind, but none of them was passionate, none of them was boiling over with outrage at social injustice. Now that leadership had passed from the pioneering founders to Yoav and his friends, the kibbutz was doomed to slide slowly into the petty bourgeoisie. And the women, of course, would be the catalyst for that process. In another twenty or thirty years, kibbutzim would become nothing more than well-kept garden communities populated by homeowners replete with material pleasures.

Yoav said, 'It's like this. Lately, some members have come to me about you. And the Health Committee sent Leah Shindlin to talk to me. The doctor told her that you must absolutely not work in the shop anymore, and we all agree with him. This shed is airless and stifling and the smells of the leather and the glue are definitely bad for your health. The entire kibbutz thinks that you've worked enough, Martin. It's time for you to rest now.'

Martin removed the oxygen mask, took a crumpled half cigarette out of his pocket, lit it with a trembling hand, inhaled and choked.

'And who will work in the shop? You, maybe?'

'We've already found a temporary replacement for you. There's a shoemaker from Romania who lives in the new immigrant camp nearby. He's unemployed. Morally speaking, Martin, we really should give him a job here and provide him with the means to support his family.

'Another paid employee? Another nail in the coffin of the principle of self-reliance?'

'Only until we find a member who can replace you.'

Martin crushed the cigarette carefully on the top of his shoemaker's bench, shook off the black ash and put the butt in his shirt pocket, coughed and wheezed, but didn't put the oxygen mask back on. A sarcastic look came over his grey-stubbled face.

'And what about me?' he said with a half-smile, 'I'm finished? Kaput? Ready for the trash heap?'

'You,' Yoav said, putting his hand on Martin's shoulder, 'you can come to the office and work with me an hour or two every morning. Organise the papers. We've decided that from now on, we're keeping all the documents that come to the secretary's office. Not exactly an archive, but something like it. Let's call it the seed of a future archive. You'll file the material in the office. Far from the suffocating air of this shed.'

Martin Vandenberg picked up a dusty work shoe with a torn sole, carefully placed it upside down on the last, spread thick, acrid-smelling glue on the inside of the sole, took a few small nails from a box on his bench and attached the sole to the shoe with five or six short, accurate blows of a small hammer.

'How can you suddenly throw a man out of work against his will only because his health is failing,' Martin said in a low voice as if he were talking to himself and not to Yoav. 'Such a Darwinistic crime is unthinkable here.'

'We're just worried about you, Martin. We all want what's best for you. And the decision is actually the doctor's, not ours.'

Martin Vandenberg did not reply to that. There was a small, pedal-operated sewing machine on his left, and he used it to sew a torn sandal. He ran the needle over the strap twice, then reinforced the spot he'd sewn with a small metal staple and put the repaired sandal on the shelf behind him. Yoav Carni stood up, gently moved the oxygen tank back onto the crate he'd been sitting on and said hesitantly, 'There's no rush. Just think about it, Martin. We're begging you to consider our suggestion. Or more accurately, our request. Remember that all of us here only want what's best for you. And organising the archive in the office for an hour or two every morning is also work. After all, don't forget that it's the prerogative of the kibbutz institutions to move a member from one job to another when they see fit.'

As he was leaving, Yoav repeated hesitantly, 'Don't be in a hurry to give us your answer. Think about it for a day or two. Rationally.'

Martin Vandenberg didn't think about Yoav's suggestion; nor did he give his answer a day or two later or a month later. His breathing grew worse, but he didn't give up his half-a-cigarette. To Osnat, who brought him a covered plate and a covered cup from the dining hall every evening, he said, 'Man is basically good and generous and decent. It's the environment that corrupts us.'

Osnat said, 'But what is the environment if not other people?'

Martin said, 'During the war, I hid from the Nazis, Osnat, but I saw them close up a few times. Simple men, not at all monsters, a bit infantile, noisy, liked to joke around, played the piano, fed the small cats, but they'd been brainwashed. And that brainwashing was the only reason they did terrible things even though they themselves weren't terrible. They'd been ruined. Corrupt ideas had ruined them.'

Osnat said nothing. She thought there was much more cruelty in the world than compassion and sometimes even compassion was a form of cruelty. Then she played three or four tunes on her recorder, said goodnight

171

and took the tray with the supper that Martin had barely touched. She thought that cruelty was deeply ingrained in all of us, and even Martin had some measure of it in him, at least towards himself. But she found no point in disagreeing with him because he was happy in his beliefs and because he had probably never deliberately harmed anyone. Osnat knew that Martin was ill and declining. She'd spoken to the doctor, who told her that his condition would not improve, and when breathing became impossible for him, they'd have to move him to the hospital. Leah Shindlin, on behalf of the Health Committee, suggested that they allocate four hours a week to Osnat from her work schedule to take care of Martin, but Osnat said that she took care of him anyway out of friendship, and there was no need for compensation. The evening hours she spent with the sick man, their brief conversations, his gratitude, the world of ideals and thought he opened to her — she treasured them all and trembled at the idea that their relationship might end soon.

★   ★   ★

Osnat hung an announcement written in Martin's spiky handwriting on the bulletin board at the entrance to the dining hall:

To the interested: Every Wednesday between six and seven in the evening, a beginners' course in Esperanto, taught by Martin V. will be held in the social club.

Esperanto is a new, easy language aimed at uniting all of humanity and becoming at least the second language of all people. Its grammar is simple and logical, it has no exceptions, and you can begin speaking and writing it after only a few lessons. Those of you who are interested can write your names at the bottom of this page.

Three people signed up: the first was Osnat herself, followed by Zvi Provizor and finally the high school junior, Moshe Yashar. On Wednesday Martin pushed his oxygen tank as he shuffled along to the social club to teach his first Esperanto lesson. Osnat walked with him and tried to take his arm gently, but he pulled away from her and insisted on making his own way. He dragged his feet, stopped from time to time, short of breath on the upward slopes, but he was determined, and reached the club some ten minutes early. He sat down to wait for his students and smoked half a cigarette, breathed through his oxygen mask, browsed the evening papers briefly and found only savagery and ugliness in them,

173

along with a heaped dose of brainwashing. Osnat poured him a cup of tea from the samovar that stood in the corner, and Martin placed his thick, gnarled fingers on the back of her left hand for a moment. Her hand was delicate and long-fingered, and the band of paler skin where her wedding ring had been before she took it off, when Boaz left her, was still visible. She pulled her hand out from under his and placed it on top. They sat that way in silence for a few moments, her fingers covering his, with their blue, oxygen-deprived nails, until the door opened and Zvi Provizor entered. He mumbled good evening and sat down in a corner next to the radio, his back rounded, his sunburned, furrowed face bent towards his knees, and waited silently. Martin complimented him on the kibbutz garden and Osnat added, 'I especially love the grape trellises and the fountain you built in the dining-hall square. You've made Kibbutz Yekhat a lovely place to stroll through.'

Zvi thanked them both and said that the trouble was some youngsters here who take shortcuts through the lawns right after they've been watered and ruin them. As he said that, Moshe Yashar came in and asked politely if the lesson was only for kibbutz members or could high school students also join. Martin Vandenberg said, 'We have no borders or limits. We are against borders in principle.'

Martin coughed and began the lesson with a short explanation: 'When all human beings speak the same language, there will be no more wars because their common language will prevent misunderstanding among individuals and peoples.' Zvi Provizor remarked that the German Jews spoke the same language as the Germans, but that didn't prevent the Germans from hunting them down and murdering them. Moshe Yashar raised his hand timidly and when Martin called on him pointed out that Cain and Abel probably spoke the same language too. Martin asked him why, if that was true, he'd come there to learn Esperanto. The boy didn't answer immediately. Finally, he mumbled submissively that learning Esperanto might help him learn other languages later on.

Martin smoked half a cigarette, wheezed, coughed deeply again and explained that Esperanto has no more than about eight thousand root words, and all the necessary vocabulary is derived from these. The roots themselves are taken from Greek and from Latin languages. There are exactly sixteen grammatical rules, with no irregularities or exceptions. At the end of the first lesson, which went on for twenty-five minutes,

Martin taught his students how to say the first verse of Genesis in Esperanto: *En la komenco Dio kreis la ĉielon kaj la teron.* In the beginning God created the heaven and the earth.

Zvi Provizor, who in his free time still translated works by the Polish writer Iwaszkiewicz into Hebrew, thought for a moment, then said that Esperanto really did seem easy and logical and sounded a bit like Spanish to him. Moshe Yashar wrote everything down in his notebook. Martin said that imprecise words poison relations between people everywhere, and that's why clear, accurate words can heal those relationships, but only if they are the right words spoken in a language that all people can understand. Moshe Yashar said nothing, but thought that the sorrow in the world was born long before words. And when Martin used the phrase 'no compromises', it occurred to Moshe that even Martin's decision to smoke the occasional half cigarette and not a whole one was actually a compromise.

After the lesson, Osnat walked Martin and the pram holding his oxygen tank back home. He was very tired, his body ached and his breathing was so laboured that he decided to forgo the half-cigarette he'd planned to smoke later that evening. Osnat was barely able to convince him to eat some yoghurt; then she helped him take off his shoes and sit down on the bed, with his back leaning against several pillows, to wait for sleep that might or might not come. After playing two songs on her recorder for him, she said goodnight, took the dinner tray and placed it on the porch steps, then went out for her evening walk along the cypress-lined avenue. At night, she heard him coughing through the thin wall that separated their beds, but as she was putting on her robe to go and check on him, the coughing stopped and didn't start up again until morning.

★   ★   ★

The second Esperanto lesson was postponed because a day before it was scheduled to take place, Martin Vandenberg's condition worsened and he was taken to the hospital in an ambulance and placed in an oxygen tent in the intensive care unit. During morning visiting hours, Leah Shindlin, as representative of the Health Committee, sat at his bedside, and in the afternoon, Osnat took her place. Martin's eyes were closed most of the time. He would occasionally mumble something or smile. His eyes looked sunken and his steel-wool hair was unkempt. When spoken to, he just nodded. Several times, he managed to say some words of thanks to the women who watched over him. In the late afternoon, he complained that he didn't have the strength to focus his thoughts. And once, when two brisk nurses came in to change his pyjamas, he grinned suddenly and told them that death itself was an anarchist. 'Death is not awed by status, possessions, power or titles; we are all equal in its eyes.' The words were fragmented and indistinct, but Osnat, who was sitting beside him, understood him and felt how precious Martin was to her; she had to find a way to tell him that now. But the words didn't come, so she merely held his warm fingers between her small, cold hands.

Five days later, his lungs stopped absorbing the oxygen that flowed into them, and he choked to death. Osnat, who was sitting beside him, stroked his forehead lightly and closed his eyes before she went out to the phone in the corridor to call Yoav Carni and tell him. Yoav sent a van with a driver to bring Osnat back home and transport the body to the kibbutz clubhouse, where, covered with a black sheet, it remained all night until the funeral the next morning. On the bulletin board in the dining hall, Yoav hung a small notice that he had pecked out with one finger on the office typewriter:

Our friend Martin Vandenberg passed away this evening.

The funeral will be held tomorrow morning at ten.

If anyone knows whether Martin has any relatives, please let Yoav know as soon as possible.

No relatives were found and only the members of Kibbutz Yekhat attended the funeral. It was a soft, blue morning and the mourners were not bothered by the heat because a pleasant breeze blowing in from the west cooled their skin. The tops of the cypress trees that encircled the cemetery trembled slightly in the breeze. A swarm of butterflies fluttered in the air, bearing the smells of the fields, the orchards and a distant fire. Fifty or sixty kibbutz members were there, all wearing their work clothes, as the funeral was taking place on a work day. They stood around the open grave and waited. There was no religious ceremony because Martin had left the Social Committee a note asking to be buried without a cantor or prayers.

David Dagan, the teacher, said a few words in the name of all the members. He described Martin Vandenberg as an anarchist who lived his entire life according to his beliefs. 'Until almost his last day,' David Dagan said,

'Martin worked in the shoe-repair shop as if he had taken upon himself symbolic responsibility for every step we took.'

Then Yoav Carni, representing the secretariat, gave a short eulogy. He pointed out that Martin had been alone all his life, a survivor who had hidden in Holland during the Holocaust. 'He saw with his own eyes how low human beings could sink, but still he came to us imbued with belief in people and in a future burning with the bright flame of justice. We were often surprised,' Yoav said, 'at his honesty and devotion to his ideals. He was an intellectual and also a man who believed in the importance of physical labour, a man of principle and of uncompromising hard work.' Then Yoav spoke in praise of Osnat, who had tended to Martin devotedly when he was sick, and ended his speech with the hope that Martin Vandenberg and all he stood for would continue to be a source of inspiration for us all.

After the eulogies, at Yoav's request Osnat played one of Martin's favourite songs on her recorder. Some of the mourners hummed quietly along with her and others just moved their lips.

Zvi Provizor, Nahum Asherov and Roni Shindlin, together with several other members, shovelled earth onto the cover of the coffin. The earth raised dust as it hit the coffin with a dry, hollow sound. Roni Shindlin stumbled on the mound of earth and would have fallen if David Dagan hadn't grabbed him by the arm and steadied him. Osnat thought about the word 'uncompromising' that Yoav had used to describe the deceased and decided she didn't like it. Nevertheless, she had warm feelings for everyone present at the funeral, and though she didn't know where that warmth stemmed from, she knew she would feel it for a long time to come.

The coffin was now completely covered and a small cloud of dust hovered over the new grave. Roni Shindlin said, 'That's it.' Then added, 'It's a real shame he's gone. There aren't many people like him left.'

He collected the five shovels they'd used to fill the grave, loaded them onto a small wheelbarrow and turned to go. The other mourners followed him, leaving the cemetery in small groups that broke up as each person went to his place of work. David Dagan reminded Moshe that the next lesson would begin in fifteen minutes. And he left. Moshe waited two or three minutes and he too left. Osnat lingered for a while beside the small mound of earth and listened to the chirping of the birds and the rattle of a distant tractor, and she felt a sense of peace, as if this hadn't been a funeral but a good, satisfying conversation. A sudden desire came over her to say one or two quiet words in Esperanto, but she hadn't had time to learn anything and she had no idea what to say.

We do hope that you have enjoyed reading this large print book.

Did you know that all of our titles are available for purchase?

We publish a wide range of high quality large print books including:
**Romances, Mysteries, Classics
General Fiction
Non Fiction and Westerns**

Special interest titles available in large print are:
**The Little Oxford Dictionary
Music Book
Song Book
Hymn Book
Service Book**

Also available from us courtesy of Oxford University Press:
**Young Readers' Dictionary
(large print edition)
Young Readers' Thesaurus
(large print edition)**

For further information or a free brochure, please contact us at:
**Ulverscroft Large Print Books Ltd.,
The Green, Bradgate Road, Anstey,
Leicester, LE7 7FU, England.
Tel:** (00 44) **0116 236 4325
Fax:** (00 44) **0116 234 0205**

Other titles published by
The House of Ulverscroft:

GOSSIP

Beth Gutcheon

Loviah French owns a boutique dress shop in Manhattan. She has two best friends: Dinah, a columnist covering New York's wealthiest; and Avis, a prominent figure in the art world. Despite the deep affection they both feel for Loviah, Dinah and Avis have been allergic to one another since an incident decades earlier — an incident that has been remembered and resented. But when a marriage means that Dinah and Avis must set aside their differences, Loviah has to manage her two friends' secrets as wisely as she can. Which is not wisely enough, as things turn out — a fact that will have a shattering effect on all their lives . . .